After our capture by the Romans, we were taken to the camp of Germanicus, and he looked us over. His wife, Agrippina, was there with a little brat about four years old hanging onto her tunic.

Suddenly the brat tugged at his mother and said, "I want," pointing at me. A centurion was about to lead us away, when Agrippina stopped him with an imperious gesture. "Hold! Caligula wishes the young barbarian. Take it away, burn that filthy wolf skin it is wearing, scrub it, and bring it to my tent."

I saw my mother's lip tremble, but she kept her head up. Father didn't even flick an eyelash. I never saw them again but for the one time in Rome. I then dedicated my life to one purpose—vengeance.

Someday I would kill a Caesar.

A SPECIAL ANNOUNCEMENT TO ALL
ERB ENTHUSIASTS

Because of the widespread, continuing interest in the books of Edgar Rice Burroughs, we are listing below the names and addresses of various ERB fan club magazines. Additional information may be obtained from the editors of the magazines themselves.

—The Editors

ERB-DOM
Rt. 2, Box 119
Clinton, LA 70722

ERBANIA
8001 Fernview Lane
Tampa, Florida 33615

TBN (THE BURROUGHS NEWSBEAT)
5813 York Avenue South
Edina, Minnesota 55410

I
AM A
BARBARIAN

BY

EDGAR RICE BURROUGHS

SF
ace books
A Division of Charter Communications Inc.
A GROSSET & DUNLAP COMPANY
51 Madison Avenue
New York, New York 10010

Printed in U.S.A.

In this free translation of the memoirs of Britannicus, for twenty-five years the slave of Caius Caesar Caligula, emperor of Rome from A.D. 37 to 41, we have deemed it expedient to use the modern rather than the ancient names of places for the purpose of clarity: Kent for Cantium, Dover for Dubris, Capri for Capreæ, et cetera.

To determine the historical accuracy of the document, the following works were consulted:

History of England by George Macaulay Trevelyan.

Caesar's Commentaries.

Lives of the Twelve Caesars by Gaius Suetonius Tranquillus.

The Tragedy of the Caesars by S. Baring-Gould.

The Early Empire by W. W. Capes.

Travel Among the Ancient Romans by William West Mooney.

The Private Life of the Romans by Harriet Waters Preston and Louise Dodge.

Rome and the Romans by Grant Showerman.

Life in the Roman World by T. G. Tucker.

The Roman Empire by H. Stuart Jones.

Roman Society by Samuel Dill.

Women of the Caesars by Guglielmo Ferrero.

The Private Life of the Romans by Harold Whetstone Johnston.

We have retained the Roman dating that appears throughout the manuscript; but, for the convenience of the reader, the corresponding years, according to modern calculation, appear at the head of each chapter.

THE EDITORS

Chapter I

✠   ✠

MY FATHER was a rugged individualist. He was about as subservient to discipline as a brown bear in the rutting season, and as for tribute: Jove! His face turned purple under its blue paint when emissaries came from Tagulus to demand it. With a single stroke of his blade, he lopped off the head of one of them and then sent it back to Tagulus by the other, saying, "Here is the only tribute that the grandson of Cingetorix pays to his enemies." In his little world there were three scourges: Pestilence, Famine, and Father.

What a man he was! I can see him now in his war chariot, lashing his horses toward the enemy, his skin stained blue, the hair of his wolf-skin tunic fluttering in the breeze, his great mustachios streaming out behind, his wolf-head helmet clamped low above his brow. Never forget, my son, that the blood of this proud barbarian flows in your veins.

From the time I was eight I rode with him. When he and his warriors leaped out with their great swords among the enemy, I followed, so that if they were hard pressed they could leap to the pole and run back between the horses and thus regain the chariot. Then we would wheel and go racing away.

My father was chief of a small tribe. He had, perhaps, a hundred fighting men, but with these he fought his way down from the north to the lush plains of Kent. Not that he particularly wished to go to Kent but that the more powerful tribes that he was constantly attacking chased him down.

The first Cingetorix had been king of Kent; but one of his younger sons, the father of my father, had gone north to raid and loot; and he had done so well that he had remained there, more or less of a scourge upon the country which he afflicted. He was one of the reasons why Father was driven south; Father was the other one.

We were not welcome in Kent. The inhabitants were most inhospitable, and we got word that Tagulus was coming down with an army of a thousand warriors to inquire why Father had lopped off the head of his emissary; so father decided to invade the Continent. He stole a couple of ships in the harbor at Dover and loaded us all aboard, warriors, women and children, and set out to conquer the Belgians.

I think he had never heard, nor had I at that time, that Julius Caesar, in writing of the inhabitants of Gaul, had said: "Of all these, the Belgae are the bravest." Not that that would have made any difference to Father, perhaps; but it might have impelled him to greater caution in his campaign of conquest.

But this is not the story of my father, though a fat volume of war, rapine, and murder could be written around the tumultous years of his manhood. It is the story of Little Boots, as told by the slave who was attached to his imperial person from his fourth year until his death.

Suffice it to say that my father did not conquer the Belgians. What was left of the tribe, and that was not much, the Belgians sold into slavery to the Chatti, a German tribe. The Germans are a very different people from us Britons. Like us, they are large men; but whereas we shave our entire bodies except our heads and upper lips, they are all covered with hair like animals. So densely are they covered with this matted mass that they always gave me the impression of peering out from ambush. Also, they stink. I am sure that not one of them has ever taken a bath for at least five generations back.

We were house guests of the Chatti in their mud huts for but a brief period, although however brief, far too long, for we were not the only tenants of their mud huts. Besides the Chatti, there were other vermin, which crawled out of their hair and swarmed upon us, upon the assumption, I presume, that fresh pastures seem the greenest. It was during those days (and nights) that I acquired that violent dislike for Germans that I have never overcome, nor tried to.

Then the Chatti were set upon and overwhelmed by Roman legions, and once again the grandson of Cingetorix and his family changed hands. The change was not for the worse, for the Romans were clean and they had food, being powerful enough to take it from one and sundry wherever they chanced to be.

The Roman general into whose hands we had passed was named Germanicus. He was the nephew and adopted son of the Emperor Tiberius, and a grand fellow withal, but not much of a military phenomenon. He was also something of a weak sister at one minute and a bloody tyrant at the next, but I think his wife sicked him on to these latter extravagances. This Agrippina was a bitch.

After our capture, we were taken to the camp of Germanicus, and he looked us over. He was greatly taken with the appearance of Father. "This," he said, pointing at him, "is a gift from the gods. He is going to be nothing less than a sensation when he is led through Rome in chains behind my chariot on the occasion of my triumph. I wish I had a couple of dozen more of him, for it is going to be too bad to have to mar the grandeur of the occasion with a lot of lousy Germans who look like gorillas and smell like mephitis. Send him and these others to Ravenna, and we shall pick them up on our way back to Rome."

Agrippina was there, eyeing us down her long nose, and there was a little brat about four years old hanging onto her tunic. He was all tricked out in the uniform of a legionary, with tiny military sandals that laced well above his ankles. He kept casting a mean eye on me.

I was standing close to my mother and my father, and we were all standing very straight and stiff as became Britons—no servile bending of the knee of the grandson of Cingetorix and his family.

Suddenly the brat tugged at his mother's tunic and said, "I want," pointing at me. I was ten years old then, and, if I do say it myself, one of the finest-looking lads it has ever been my privilege to encounter.

A centurion was about to lead us away, when Agrippina stopped him with an imperious gesture; and, believe me, you don't know what an imperious gesture is unless you have seen Agrippina unleash one.

"Hold!" said Agrippina. "Caligula wishes the young barbarian. Take it away, burn that filthy wolf skin it is wearing, scrub it, and bring it to my tent."

I saw my mother's lip tremble, but she kept her head up and looked straight to the front. Father didn't even flick an eyelash, and his great mustachios looked as fierce as ever. I never saw them again but once: that was in Rome. I never spoke with either of my parents again.

I was now the slave of Little Boots, as the legionaries had named him because of the caligae that he wore. He was their darling, and I will say that at that time he was a very cute kid. They were so fond of him that a little later, when Agrippina was supposed to return to Rome because she was about to bring another nitwit into the world, the soldiers would not let Little Boots go with her; and Agrippina and Germanicus had to bow to their will.

These Roman soldiers were not such a bad lot when you got to know them. The veterans were tough, and fine soldiers; but Germanicus had a lot of conscripts drafted from the slums of Rome and old soldiers who had been dragged from their farms. The former wished to get back to Rome, the latter back to their farms; and they all wanted money and loot. They were a spoiled lot; and the officers, all the way up to the commanding general, were afraid of them.

Shortly after we were brought to the camp, four legions mutinied and demanded that Germanicus lead them back to Rome and dispute the throne with Tiberius, but Germanicus refused. Many of the veterans tried to play upon his sympathies by a display of infirmities of age. I saw one old fellow seize the hand of Germanicus as though to kiss it and then stick the general's fingers in his mouth to feel his toothless gums; another exposed his legs, crippled with rheumatism, while others uncovered their skinny shanks, shriveled from old age. The younger men milled around, blustering and threatening.

Germanicus was a good soul, kindly and generous, but he was never cut out to command Roman legions. As I watched him that day, I could not but visualize what Father would have done under like circumstances; he would have waded in single-handed with that great sword of his and licked four legions or died in the attempt.

But Germanicus pleaded. He tried to play upon their sympathies. It is hard to believe of one who might have expected someday to be emperor of Rome, but I was there and witnessed it with my own eyes and ears.

"Rather will I die than forget my duty," he cried, and then he drew his sword. "Return to your duties, or I shall plunge this into my heart."

Several soldiers threw their arms about him to prevent this, but others encouraged him contemptuously. "Go to it!" cried several, and one who had been a gladiator drew his own sword and offered it to Germanicus with a sneer. "Take this," he said. "You will find it sharper than your own!"

Seeing that their general was making a damn fool of himself, Caius Caetronius and several other officers surrounded him and hurried him off to his tent.

This was my introduction to the ruling family of

Rome and the much vaunted Roman legions. Years of association with them have not tended to improve the opinion I then formed as a little boy of ten; in fact, quite the reverse.

This is not the story of my father, neither is it a history of Rome; but I am constrained to mention a couple of incidents which helped to fix first impressions indelibly in the plastic mind of a boy. Germanicus had met with two serious defeats at the hands of the Germans; and to retrieve lost prestige he undertook another campaign, in fact two of them. In these he lost practically all of a large fleet of ships and fully half of his army; but he took a few poor villages; and, upon the strength of this, pompous boasts of his successes were relayed to Rome.

The Emperor Tiberius, a great general himself, was also a wise old fox. He read between the lines; and to prevent Germanicus from losing the rest of his army, he recalled him to Rome to enjoy his triumph.

For two small boys, the life in a Roman camp close beside a German forest was about as close an approximation of heaven as one may ever expect to attain on earth. It was a mysterious forest, dark and forbidding, in whose depths might lurk sprites and nymphs and demons and strange, wild beasts such as only a boy of ten can conjure irrefutably from the crystal-clear depths of a budding imagination.

I knew our own oak forests of Briton, and I knew

names of the sprites and nymphs and demons who lived in them, though I had seen relatively few of these. But I had seen the great herds of wild swine, the wolves, the bears, and the red deer, and I had known of more than one hunter who had entered these forests and never returned. Yet the forests of Briton seemed friendly, like the fierce face of my father, because I knew them so well; but the German forest was different. However, I did not fear it, being, as I am, the son of my father and the great-grandson of Cingetorix, neither of whom ever knew fear.

Be all that as it may, I did not enter the forest beside which we were camped, because they would not let me. And they would not let me because Little Boots would never let me out of his sight, and, naturally, they would not permit the four-year-old grandnephew of the emperor to expose his divine person to the attention of sprites and nymphs and demons, to say nothing of sundry savage and perpetually ravenous beasts. When I was quite certain that I could not obtain permission to enter the forest, I begged persistently to do so until Agrippina handed me one with the flat of her hand on the side of my head that sent me spinning. The result would have been little different had I been kicked by a mule, a beast of which Agrippina always reminded me.

I have already mentioned my introduction to the lady. After I had been made to take a bath, which I did not need, being already fully as clean as members of the imperial family, I was given sandals and a tunic which did not fit me, they having been designed for a legionary, and escorted back to the tent of Germanicus, from which rose screams and howls of a most astounding volume. Especially astounding were they when I discovered that they proceeded from the lungs of a four-year-old child.

Agrippina met me at the entrance. "Come here, you nasty little barbarian," she commanded. Then she turned toward the interior of the tent. "Here he is," she snapped. "Now for the love of Jove, stop your bawling."

At sight of me, Little Boots immediately stopped yelling and grinned at me. There was not a tear in his eye: he had just known how to get what he wanted, and I suppose he wanted me because there were no other children in the camp and he longed for a playfellow. There were some women in the camp but no other children that I ever saw. The women were quartered down below the lines where the cavalry horses and sumpter mules were tethered, and they were not allowed to move freely about the camp, nor were Little Boots and I permitted to approach that part of the camp. I did sneak down there once when Little Boots was taking a nap, but after I saw a number of the ladies and heard their conversation, I understood why they had been segregated.

As any bright child would have done, I picked up

the language of my captors quickly. I had to, for I heard nothing else. The first speeches that I heard and which in any way referred to me, I carried fairly well in my memory, so that I soon had the gist of them and was later able to render a rather free translation of them, which I have previously set down in these memoirs. Among the first words that I picked up (and what boy would not have?), were the robust oaths of the soldiers: within a week of my coming, I could curse like a legionary.

All my life I had had a very good name of which I was quite proud, but Agrippina did not even inquire as to what it might be. No. After the custom of the Romans, she gave me a brand new name as they do to all slaves. She named me Britannicus Caligulae Servus. The Britannicus was given me either in derision or because of my origin: I neither knew nor cared. It was a fine, full sounding name, and I liked it. From the beginning, Little Boots called me Brit, and thenceforth I was Brit to him, the members of his household, his intimates, and my own friends; but not to Agrippina. To her I was Britannicus, that Vile Barbarian, or just plain Servus.

I do not know why she took such a violent dislike to me, unless it was due to unconscious jealousy, aroused by the childish passion of Little Boots for me.

She was a terrible woman: proud, arrogant, dictatorial, jealous, cruel. She looked with thinly veiled contempt, or with open contempt, upon all in whose veins did not flow the divine blood of the Julii, even thus upon her husband, who was of the Claudian branch of the family.

Her pride in the Julian blood stemmed from the fact that the family was supposed to have descended directly from a goddess: Venus. But why that should have been anything to boast of, I do not know. Had I been descended from Venus, I should have kept the matter very quiet. She had been a notoriously loose woman, appallingly promiscuous. There was still another and more vital reason why I should never have announced the fact from the housetops: the moral turpitude and mental disorder of the line which was quite apparent even to many of the Julians. Julius Caesar was an epileptic; Agrippina's mother, Julia, was a notorious wanton and adulteress; so was Agrippina's sister, Julia; her brother, Agrippa Posthumus, was a madman; her other brothers, Caius and Lucius, were weak and sickly, dying young, the former insane before his death; and from my earliest experiences of the woman, I felt, even as a small boy, that she was mentally unbalanced: her appalling fits of rage, her total lack of ability to control her temper attested the fact.

This, then, was the Julian line, worshipped as semidivine. The Claudians were only scrofulous.

I have digressed from the story of Little Boots that I might roughly paint in a portion of the backdrop against which his short life was played.

The first night that I spent in the Roman camp, I was sent off to sleep in a tent with other slaves, where I presently heard shrieks and screams coming from the general direction of the tents of Germanicus. They sounded somewhat as if a small child were being burnt at the stake.

"That brat is at it again," grumbled one of the slaves.

"What do you suppose he wants now?"

"Probably the moon."

"Well, that is about the only thing the old she-wolf can't get him."

Presently a slave came puffing to our tent. He looked in, and by the light of the small oil lamp that was burning, he finally espied me. "Come with me, slave," he said, although he was a slave himself: just putting on airs.

It was not the moon that Little Boots wished: it was I.

Agrippina was furious. "Oh, there you are, you nasty little barbarian; and it's about time. You will sleep there," she pointed at a mattress that had been placed at the foot of Little Boot's cot.

Little Boots stopped screaming and grinned at me. "Hello there, Brit!" he said drowsily and fell asleep. After that, I slept either at the foot of his bed or just outside his door until the day of his death.

Never shall I forget that first night in the Roman camp on the Rhine. In all my ten years I had never

seen a village which contained more than a couple
of hundred souls, and here I was in a camp laid out
with military precision, with streets and row upon
row of tents, lighted by flaring torches, and containing fully seventy-five thousand men.

As I lay at the foot of the cot of the little Caesar,
my ears wide with wonder, I listened to the night
sounds of a Roman camp: the sentries calling the
hours; now the neighing of a horse at the picket
line, and the thin laughter of women, far away; the
attenuated notes of a lute, haunting, provocative,
mysterious, coming wanly as though from a great
distance, perhaps from the depths of the black and
threatening forest my imagination would have it;
raucous laughter, oaths, terrific quarreling from the
tents of the legionaries; querulous nagging from the
tent of Agrippina and Germanicus.

The Romans are not a tall race—my father had
towered above them—but their great numbers, their
loud boastings, their terrific oaths metamorphosed
them into giants in my small mind; and I lay on my
mattress and trembled as I thought what my fate
might be among them. Of them all, I thought,
Agrippina was the most terrible. With far greater
equanimity, I could have faced the seventy-five
thousand legionaries. I was almost afraid then; but
suddenly I recalled that I was the great-grandson of
Cingetorix; and I was not afraid, even though I
well knew that only the bawling of a small brat
stood between me and sudden death. I was wonder-

ing if Little Boots would continue to bawl at just the correct psychological moments, when I fell asleep.

My duties consisted in tagging Little Boots around and playing with him. In some ways he seemed much older than he actually was, due, possibly, to the fact that people of this southern clime mature more rapidly than do we Britons, as well as to his exclusively adult companionships. He never talked "baby-talk," a form of linguistic aberration for which doting mothers are largely responsible and to which he was never exposed. One might as easily have conceived of Cingetorix playing with dolls as of Agrippina talking baby-talk. The result was that Little Boots was addicted to words and forms of speech often several sizes too large for him. He was a pretty nice little kid, only terribly spoiled. Even at this early age his mother had succeeded in impressing upon his childish mind that he was a Julian, the grandnephew of the emperor of the world, and that everyone else was scum put on earth merely to do the bidding of Julians and to be spit upon if they felt so inclined.

When he became vexed with me, he would call me a vile barbarian, taking the cue from his sainted mother. Once he spit on me and I slapped him down. I did not at the time realize that I was slapping down a future emperor of Rome; though, had I done so, it would have made no difference, for even future emperors of Rome cannot spit on the

great-grandson of Cingetorix with impunity. We are
a proud line, neither insane nor scrofulous.

He started screaming that time and ran in search
of Agrippina. I made my way rather hurriedly to
the picket lines and insinuated myself between two
very large cavalry horses. I was there but a short
time when I heard a most unusual commotion about
the camp: men were running in all directions—
tribunes, centurions, and common legionaries.

Perhaps, I thought, the Germans are about to
attack us. I hoped so, but it was nothing so nice as
that. They were looking for me, as I had more than
half suspected, though I tried not to admit it.
Presently one of them found me: it was Tibur, the
legionary who had been a gladiator, the one who
had offered his sword to Germanicus that time the
general had threatened to kill himself.

"Oh-ho!" he exclaimed. "So there you are! What
did you do, kid? The old bitch is raring around like
a horse with the colic and threatening to have you
skinned alive. What in hell *did* you do?"

"He spit on me," I said.

"And you?"

"I slapped him down."

"Good boy!" cried Tibur, slapping me on the
back. "She'll have you killed for it, but it's worth it.
Now, come along with me. I hate to do it, but
there's no sense in both of us being killed."

Tibur led me back to the tent of Germanicus. He
was there, and Agrippina, and Caius Caetronius,

and Little Boots. Little Boots made a face and stuck his tongue out at me.

Agrippina was trembling all over. "Did you dare strike Caius Caesar, you vile barbarian?" she demanded.

"No, ma'am," I replied, "but I slapped Little Boots' face. He spit on me." I had never heard Caligula's real name before, so I didn't know whom she was talking about, and it occurred to me that maybe it wouldn't go so hard with me if I had only slapped Little Boots rather than Caius Caesar; that Caesar sounded impressive.

Agrippina was so angry that she could scarcely speak, but she finally found her voice. "Take him out and have him beaten to death," she said to Tibur.

Little Boots began to scream. Germanicus put an end to that with a curt command. "Wait!" he said to Tibur, and then he turned again to Little Boots. "Did you spit on Britannicus?" he asked.

"Yes," said Little Boots. "He is my slave; I can spit on him if I choose."

"A gentleman does not do such things," said Germanicus, gravely, "much less a prince of the imperial house."

Agrippina stamped her foot. "Why all this foolishness?" she demanded. "Take the creature out and beat it to death!"

"I can die," I said. "I am the great-grandson of Cingetorix."

Little Boots began to scream again. "No! No! No!" he cried. "I want Brit."

"You may go," said Germanicus to Tibur. So I was not beaten to death, nor do I know whether it was Little Boots or Germanicus who saved me. After this, Agrippina was no fonder of me. I can sometimes see those terrible, malevolent eyes of hers upon me in my sleep.

After this episode, Little Boots and I took up the more or less even tenor of our ways just as if nothing had occurred to rift the lute, for such is the easy accommodation of childhood to the amenities of its little life. But Little Boots never spit on me again; and up to the day of his death, even when he was master of the world, he seemed just a little bit afraid of me. From the day of his birth to the day of his death, I was probably the only man who ever struck him. That blow, and it was no light one, must have made an indelible impression upon the mind of a child.

Of all the thousands of men in that Roman camp, Tibur the ex-gladiator had made the most profound impression upon me. He was a huge man of mighty muscles. In designing him, the gods seemed to have sacrificed his forehead that they might have more material for his bull neck, and they had certainly wasted little thought upon the pulchritude of his assembled features. Yet there was a certain magnificent grandeur in that face of his that compelled admiration: like Vesuvius in eruption it was magnificent because it was so terrible. To me, he was a greater man than Germanicus; he was certainly more of a man.

I used to drag Little Boots into the camp to find Tibur when he was off duty, and we would listen to his tall tales of the arena open-mouthed and goggle-eyed. It seemed that Tibur had been sentenced to the arena for murder (he was very proud of that murder and recounted it over and over again together with all the gory details); but when he killed every opponent pitted against him, including bears, lions, and tigers, Augustus pardoned him, and he became a professional gladiator. How many men and beasts he had killed he could not tell us, though I begged him to try to recall. I became inclined to believe, as I matured and came to know Tibur even better, that he could not satisfy my curiosity on this point because he could not count beyond ten. Though of gigantic stature, Tibur was no mental giant. Here again the gods had failed to maintain an equable balance.

Tibur seemed to take a great fancy to me from the day that I slapped Little Boots down, and as any little boy would have been, I was very proud of the friendship of a gladiator. Although they may have been reputed to be the scum of the earth (and they certainly were so reputed), even nobles and senators bragged of their acquaintance with successful gladiators. Tibur only tolerated Little Boots on my account.

"He can't never amount to nothin'," he confided
to me once, "with a crazy she-wolf for a mother and
a weepin' willow for a father. Anyway, we don't
have to worry about him: he won't never be emper-
or—there's too many ahead of him."

That remark opened my eyes. "Could Little
Boots ever possibly be emperor of Rome?" I demanded.

"Sure," said Tibur, "if enough people were
knifed or poisoned, he sure could—unless he was
knifed or poisoned."

After that, I looked upon Little Boots with something of awe—for about two days; then I recalled
that I was the great-grandson of Cingetorix, and
after that, Little Boots never seemed particularly
important to me.

When Little Boots was born there were five males
of Julian or Claudian blood, any one of whom might
reasonably have been expected to succeed to the
imperial purple upon the death of Tiberius rather
than this child. They were Germanicus, his father;
Agrippa Posthumus, his uncle; Nero Caesar and
Drusus Caesar, his older brothers; and Claudius,
nephew of the Emperor. In addition to these, Tiberius Gemellus, grandson of Tiberius, was born when
Little Boots was seven. So Tibur's prophecy that he
would never be emperor seemed well-founded; but
even before that, when Little Boots was two years
old, Agrippa Posthumus, the madman, was murdered by order of Emperor Augustus; and there

were more to follow. There were more ways than one to succeed to the Roman throne: there were poison and the dagger, with natural death running a poor third or not in the running at all.

But to get on with my story: I was in this camp in Germany for a year; then we all went to Rome. Germanicus was going to enjoy a triumph because he had captured a few poor mud huts.

Chapter II

✠   ✠

It was in the Year of the Founded City 770
that we arrived in Rome for the triumph of Germanicus. I was eleven years old, and I had lived all
my life among the primitive hamlets of timber,
wattles, or mud of Briton. In Germany, I had seen
sod huts even less admirable than the mean habita-
tions of my native land. On the way south, I had
marveled at Ravenna, and some of the other towns
through which we passed had filled my childish
mind with wonder; but they had not prepared me
for Rome.

From Tibur's descriptions, I thought that I had
gathered at least a hazy conception of the size and
grandeur of the Eternal City; but when it broke
upon my astounded vision, I realized that it had
been far beyond the scope of even my childish

imagination as well as Tibur's limited descriptive powers: he was much better at describing murders and gladiatorial combats.

I was struck dumb by the enormity of Rome, and I use that word in both its senses. Rome was not only vast but brutal. The villas and palaces, the temples, the baths, the amphitheater, the Forum were magnificent; but the great, close-packed rows of apartments and tenements, rearing their frowning and hideous fronts threateningly above the narrow streets—these were brutal.

In Ravenna, I had seen my first buildings of over one story, so you may imagine the effect that the tenements of Rome had upon me, towering to the full seventy-foot limit which Augustus had set. When I walked between them, I was always confident that the first high wind would topple them over upon me.

But of course you for whom these memoirs are set down upon my papyrus sheets, my son and my grandchildren, if I am ever so blessed, need no description of Rome: my only wish is to enable you to visualize the effect of this stupendous city upon a little barbarian boy.

After we arrived in Rome, we went at first to live at the villa of Antonia, the mother of Germanicus. Here, Little Boots had his hobbyhorses, his toy houses and carts, and his other childish playthings. Of course I, being eleven, was disgusted by such infantile occupations; and though I was forced to play with him, I thought to divert his interest in them to more manly amusements; so I tried to teach him to spin tops, skip stones, and walk on stilts. After we had broken a few windows with the stones and Little Boots had fallen on his face from the stilts and gotten a bloody nose, Agrippina turned thumbs down on my educational curriculum, accompanying her dictum with a healthy swipe at the side of my head, which I ducked, thereby increasing her rage to such an extent that she threw an expensive vase at me: that woman had absolutely no self-control. She should have been more physically and temperamentally restrained at a time like this, as she had been up only about a week following the birth of another ill-starred child: Drusilla, whose tragic fate I shall set down in its proper place.

As I ran from the peristyle toward the side door of the villa, I heard her remark that she would have my throat cut if she ever laid eyes on me again; and as I vanished from her sight out into the great city, I heard the screams and bawls of Little Boots shattering the peace of the world.

I was unfamiliar with Rome. I did not know where to go, which way to turn. All I was quite certain of was that I did not wish to have my throat cut. I wandered about aimlessly, wondering what I should do for food and where I was to sleep. I had to concentrate on the fact that I was the great-grandson of Cingetorix, so that I should not be afraid, but it was most difficult.

In all that great city, I had not a single friend. I was thinking this very thought when I saw a legionary swaggering along the street. Instantly I recalled Tibur: I did have a friend! But how could I find him among all these thousands of people? I remembered that before we had left the camp in Germany he had, through the centurion of his century, addressed a plea to Germanicus to be transferred to the Praetorian Guard on our return to Rome.

I ran after the legionary and plucked at his tunic. He turned around and scowled at me. "Not a copper," he said gruffly. "Get out!" Then he took another look and, evidently noticing that my clothes were too good for those of a beggar, he asked me what I wanted.

"Do you know Tibur, the gladiator?" I asked.

"That gorilla? Sure, I know him. What about him?"

"He is my friend. I wish to find him. I think he is now a member of the Praetorian Guard."

"He is, and he is at the Praetorian Camp," said the legionary.

"Where is that?" I asked.

"You mean to tell me that you don't know where the Praetorian Camp is?" he demanded. "Who are you, anyway? What is your name?"

I almost said that I was Britannicus Caligulae Servus, but just in time I realized that if I told him that he would send me packing off back to the villa of Antonia. So I just said, "I am the great-grandson of Cingetorix."

He grinned. "Now ain't that a coincidence?" he said. "Just fancy you and me meeting like this: I am the grandniece of Cleopatra."

I didn't know who Cleopatra was, but I knew that he was spoofing me, for he certainly wasn't anybody's grandniece.

"Will you please tell me how to get to the Praetorian Camp?" I asked, very politely.

"I'll do even better than that, sonny," he replied. "I'll take you there, for that's right where I'm going now."

It seemed quite a long walk to me, but we finally reached the camp, and in no time at all located Tibur.

"Here," said my guide to Tibur, "is the great-grandson of Cingetorix, come to pay you a visit," and he laughed until his sides shook.

"What are you laughing at?" demanded Tibur.

"Why, this little squirt says that he is the great-grandson of Cingetorix. Wouldn't that make anybody laugh?"

"It wouldn't make me laugh, you big baboon," said Tibur, "because he *is* the great-grandson of Cingetorix."

The other looked very crestfallen.

"And not only that," continued Tibur, "he is a man to be reckoned with. He slapped down the son of Agrippina and Germanicus and still lives. That, baboon, is more than you could do." Then he turned to me. "What are you doing here, *sonny?* In trouble again?"

"Agrippina says that if she ever lays eyes on me again she will have my throat cut."

Both the guardsmen whistled—long drawn-out, speculative whistles. The baboon, whose name was Vibiu, remarked that it might not be healthy to be found in my company. He hoped no one had seen him conducting me through the streets of Rome.

"What you been doin' now, sonny?" demanded Tibur.

"Nothing," I said. "It was Little Boots. He fell off his stilts and got a bloody nose—I was just trying to teach him to walk on them. He kept teasing me, and finally I let him try it. Agrippina threw a very nice vase at me, but I dodged it and it broke all to pieces against one of the pillars of the colonnade. It was one of Antonia's best vases," I added.

"They have had slaves burned at the stake for less than that," said Vibiu. "Why, even a patrician was sentenced to death for wearing into a latrine a ring on which was engraved a likeness of the Emperor; but Tiberius pardoned him. He would probably not bother to pardon a slave."

Tibur was in deep thought; and when Tibur was in deep thought, it was really quite painful to witness his facial contortions: he seemed to think

on the outside of his head. But perhaps this is quite
understandable when one considers that there was
not much room inside his head.

"If we don't want to end up on the Gemonian
steps ourselves," said Vibiu, "we'd better turn this
brat over to our centurian."

"No!" bellowed Tibur in a terrible voice. "And if
you tell anyone you have seen him, I'll cut your
heart out and eat it."

Just then a trumpet sounded, and Vibiu said,
"Now what in hell is that for?"

"You ought to know," growled Tibur. "The
legion is being called out, sonny," he said to me.
"I'll look after you when we're dismissed. I know a
woman in the city who will hide you until we can
make other plans." Then he and Vibiu hurried
away.

As no one knew me, I went out to where the
legion was forming, motivated by my boyish curiosity, for I knew that this must be something unusual.
It was.

The Lieutenant-General was out in front of the
legion with his aides and a civilian who was half-
hidden from me by the officers. The General began
to address the legion, and I crept around closer
where I could hear better. I just heard the last part
of his orders: ". . . and when you are within the
city, you will have your men break ranks and search
every house in Rome until you find him."

I wondered whom they were looking for: probably some great malefactor, I thought. Then I heard a sudden exclamation, and someone yelled, "There he is now!"

I looked. The man who yelled was the civilian I had half-seen among the officers. I knew him. He was Antonia's majordomo, and he was pointing at me! I turned and ran; and at a command from the General, the whole legion broke ranks and pursued me.

Believe me, I gave them a merry chase, and they never would have caught up with me had I not run plunk into a sentry who grabbed me just on general principles, although he didn't know what it was all about.

That legion was puffing when it arrived and surrounded me, and the General was puffing hardest of all and was very red in the face.

"You young jackanapes," he got out between puffs. "Why did you run away?"

"Because I didn't want my throat cut," I replied quite honestly.

Just then, the majordomo came puffing along like a grampus, in time to hear what I said.

"In the name of all the gods," he cried, "come along with me; nobody is going to cut your throat. All that they want of you is that you should get back there as quickly as possible. Little Boots has been screeching at the top of his lungs ever since you ran away, and they are afraid that he will break something in his insides. If he does, then you *will* get your throat cut. Come along!"

He grasped me by an arm and hustled me off to a carruca drawn by four horses. We were back at Antonia's in nothing flat. Little Boots was still screaming, but he stopped, perfectly dry-eyed, when I entered the tablinum—and winked at me.

Agrippina muttered something that sounded very much like "Nasty little barbarian," and flounced out of the room. There was no more stilt-walking for either Little Boots or myself: she had the stilts broken up and burned.

"That," said Little Boots, "was a dirty trick—just when I was learning to walk on them. I'm going to get even with her."

I didn't know how he planned getting even with Agrippina. I felt that it would take nothing less than the Emperor and a couple of cohorts of legionaries to give the old girl what we both thought she had coming to her—nothing, in fact, that two kids could do; but Little Boots was already resourceful in affairs of vengeance.

"Come!" he said, and led the way to the pool in the peristyle. "Help me catch a frog, Brit."

That meant that I had to catch the frog, which, of course, was no trick at all.

"What do you want of a frog?" I asked.

"Wait and see," said Little Boots. "You are going to be surprised; so will someone else."

"I don't know what you are going to do," I said, "but I think you had better not do it."

"Silence, slave!" said Little Boots.

"You call me that again and I won't play with you," I shot back.

"Well, you *are* a slave."

"I am the great-grandson of Cingetorix."

"Still, you are yet a slave, and I am a Julian. That's the same as being a god."

"Nuts!" I said. "Who ever put that silly idea in your head?"

"My mother has told me that many times. She says that I must never forget it. She also says that someday I may be emperor of Rome."

"Fat chance," I remarked. "There are too many ahead of you."

"Mother says that unfortunate accidents sometimes happen and that one can never tell. Of course, Nero and Drusus are older than I, but they might die. I wish they would. I don't like either of them."

"That is no way to speak of your brothers," I reminded him.

"They are a couple of stuck-up pip-squeaks. Come on; hide that frog in your tunic and come along with me."

I did as he bid, wondering. He led the way up to the balcony which ran around the peristyle. It was there that the bedrooms of the family were located. Little Boots sauntered along as innocent as a newly hatched robin—apparently. There seemed to be no one about but his grandmother, who was taking her afternoon siesta. You could hear her taking it from a considerable distance; she was taking it in a big way.

"Is she a goddess?" I asked, jerking my head in the direction of the room from which issued Antonia's loud snores.

"Not quite," said Little Boots, "but almost. She isn't a Julian, but she's the sister of Tiberius."

"In Britannia," I said, "we have gods and goddesses, but they don't snore."

"She is almost a Roman goddess; so she can do whatever she pleases, and if it pleases her to snore, she snores."

· He sauntered on nonchalantly and peeked into his mother's room; there was no one there. "Come on in," he invited.

"I don't want to," I told him. "If she caught me in there, she would have me skinned alive."

"Fraidy-cat," said Little Boots. "I thought you said you were the great-grandson of Cingetorix. I bet he wouldn't be afraid."

That was too much for me. "I am not afraid," I boasted, and followed him into the room.

"Have you the frog?" he asked.

"I have the frog," I replied.

"Well, put it in Mother's bed."

I could feel my hair standing on end. What horrid pathological mental process had put that hideous idea into the brat's head? "Not on your life," I said, backing away.

"Great-grandson of Cingetorix! Great-grandson of Cingetorix! Great-grandson of Cingetorix!" the imp of Hades kept repeating in a singsong taunt.

"My great-grandfather was a very brave man," I said, "but he had some brains—which I have inherited. Put the frog in her bed yourself."

"Put it in; I command you!" he said.

I told him to go and jump in the pool.

"You won't?" he demanded.

"No."

"Then I'll put it in myself, and if they suspect me, I shall say that you did it."

"And they'll cut my throat, and you won't have anyone to play with."

He thought this over, but he went and put the frog in Agrippina's bed. By that time I had fled.

Butter wouldn't have melted in Little Boots' mouth that evening at supper. He was so angelic that Germanicus was apprehensive concerning the state of his health. "What do you suppose is the matter with Caligula?" he demanded.

Everybody looked at Little Boots: his mother, his grandmother, and his two brothers, Nero and Drusus.

"Are you ill, darling?" inquired Agrippina.

"Yes," lied Little Boots.

"If the child is ill, he should not be permitted to

eat anything more today. He should be put right to bed," said Antonia.

"I'm not that ill," said Little Boots hurriedly.

As usual at mealtimes, I was standing directly behind him, and I had difficulty in suppressing a grin—a grin tempered by apprehension. I could not get that frog out of my mind.

"The little pig has probably been stealing pastries from the pantry," suggested Drusus, giving Caligula a dirty look.

"If you will look around, you will probably find that he has been drawing pictures on Grandmother's walls again," suggested Nero.

"I have not," yelled Little Boots at the top of his lungs. "I have not. But I know what you've been doing, and if you aren't careful, I'll tell. Yah!" and he stuck out his tongue at Nero. A great light burst suddenly upon my consciousness and my throat suddenly felt much safer.

"Shut up, brat!" snapped Nero.

"Children! Children!" chided Germanicus.

"Just what have you been doing, Nero?" demanded Agrippina.

"Nothing," replied Nero, sullenly; but then, as he was always sullen, this aroused no comment.

Antonia sent a slave to inspect her walls.

Supper passed off without further incident, Agrippina keeping up a steady stream of adverse criticism of practically everybody who was unfortunate enough to be mentioned and especially of the

Emperor Tiberius, principally, I gathered, due to the fact that he was descended from a line of scrofulous ancestors rather than from one that was divine, epileptic, and insane. Of course, she didn't put it exactly that way.

An hour after supper they sent Little Boots off to bed, and of course I had to go along with him. Our room was off the balcony right across the peristyle from Agrippina's, and Nero and Drusus each had a room on the same side. Being older, they were allowed to sit up later than was Little Boots. Nero was eleven then, and Drusus ten. I was just the same age as Nero, and I used to wish sometimes that I could play with him and Drusus instead of having to tag around after a baby. That was before I really got acquainted with them. After I did, I would just about as soon have played with Agrippina. They were arrogant, sullen little beasts, hating each other cordially. Drusus was especially bitter because Nero, being older, stood a better chance of some day becoming emperor. From birth, apparently, all the male children in both lines had that idea impressed upon them—to grow up and become an emperor and be poisoned or stabbed in the back. It always seemed to me a ridiculous ambition.

Personally, as long as I had to live in Rome, I preferred to be a slave; for I soon discovered that a well-behaved slave in a wealthy family was about the happiest and safest creature in the Eternal City. As soon as you started up—freedman, freeman, citizen, office holder—then someone below you started sitting up nights brewing poison or sharpening a dagger.

It took me some time to get to sleep that night. In the first place, I was too old to go to bed so early, and, in the second, I had something on my mind. And then a remark of Little Boots just before he fell asleep did not tend to quiet my nerves. He said, "You don't have to worry about having your throat cut, Brit. Mother was just talking nonsense when she said that."

"What do you mean, I don't have to worry about having my throat cut?" I asked.

"It's like this," said Little Boots. "When a slave commits a crime, we do not cut his throat; we crucify him." Then the little brat went to sleep as though his conscience were perfectly snow-white, only I think he never had any conscience. Absolute, 100 per cent selfishness and a conscience cannot abide in the same soul. Perhaps I should say in the same ego, as Caligula had no soul.

I must have fallen asleep eventually, because I was later awakened, a phenomenon which presupposes prior slumber; and *how* I was awakened! A series of terrifying shrieks and screams were fairly raising the roof from the house of Antonia; then I heard people rushing from doorways all over the place, asking "What?" and "Which?" and "Who?"

I did not have to ask what or which or who. I knew all the answers to these, and now I had the answer to one I had been asking myself just before I fell asleep: When? Knowing all the answers, I was most incurious; so I pulled the covers up over my head and lay very quiet.

Notwithstanding all the racket, Agrippina found Little Boots and me fast asleep when she came barging into our room. She kicked me, and then she shook Little Boots. We were now awake.

"Which one of you imps of Satan put that frog in my bed?" she demanded.

"What frog?" asked Little Boots.

"The frog in my bed," she snapped.

"In your bed?"

"Yes, in my bed. Was it you or this filthy little barbarian? Speak up, before I skin you both alive."

Agrippina was overwrought. Germanicus stood behind her, and Antonia, and Nero, and Drusus, with a rear guard of freedmen and slaves; also the fat little majordomo, Serenus. Some of the slaves bore torches, and in their light I could have sworn that I saw the shadow of a smile on the lips of Germanicus.

"Well?" demanded Agrippina.

Being in the presence of members of the imperial family, I had stood up as soon as Agrippina got through kicking me. I kept thinking of the slaves I had seen nailed to crosses along the Via Flaminia, and I had to concentrate on the fact that I was the great-grandson of Cingetorix to make my knees behave.

I was wondering what Little Boots would say. He said nothing—for the moment.

"Was it you, Servus?" the granddaughter of Augustus demanded, casting a mean eye on me, an eye surcharged with loathing.

"No," I said, "I would not dare."

The old girl turned that eye on Little Boots. The ball of one bare foot was tapping ominously upon the mosaic of the floor—on the rear end of a naked cherub, I recall.

"Caligula!" she barked. "You did it."

"I did not," yelled Little Boots, and he began to scream.

"That will do, Caligula!" snapped Germanicus, and that did do. Little Boots shut up.

"One of you must have done it," said Agrippina, still probing.

"We did not," said Little Boots, and I breathed again. "Nero did it." I stopped breathing.

Nero let out a yell that must have startled the sentries in the Praetorian Camp. "Shrimp! Beetle! Bedbug!" he screamed. "He lies!"

"I saw him," said Little Boots, without turning a hair. "He wanted me to do it, but I wouldn't."

"Wait 'till I get hold of you," said Nero. "I'll wring your foul neck; just wait."

"You'll do nothing of the kind," said Germanicus, "and we've had about enough of this. Get off to bed, all of you. Come on, Aggie; you're making an awful fuss over a little childish joke."

"Childish joke!" she snorted. "And how many times do I have to tell you not to call me Aggie?"

I lay awake for some time after they had gone away. I heard Agrippina stewing in her room for some little time, and the last thing I recall of that harrowing night was the snores of Antonia.

Chapter III

✠ ✠

THE NEXT day dawned clear and beautiful. A lark sang in the spacious gardens in the rear of the house of Antonia as Little Boots and I prepared to arise, eager for the great spectacle which we were to view this day—the triumph of Germanicus. The Roman sun looked down upon a Roman world; even the air was Roman air, and no cloud sullied the spotless blue of the Roman heavens—at least, not at first; then Nero Caesar burst upon our horizon, a thundercloud of the first magnitude. He appeared to be angry—quite angry, in fact; and he had a stick in his hand.

"Don't touch me!" yelled Little Boots. "Brit! Brit! Don't let him touch me! Knock his block off!"

I backed up and stood in front of Little Boots,

48

but I inwardly questioned the wisdom of knocking the block off Nero Caesar. I had learned that one does not with impunity knock the block off a Caesar, and the memory of the crucified slaves along the Via Flaminia arose to counsel me.

I thought of a better plan. Turning and stooping, I whispered to Little Boots, "Scream! Scream like hell!"

Little Boots, catching the drift of the idea, screamed. Nero's lower jaw sprung loose and dangled; his eyes popped; then he turned and vanished into the golden sunlight—and not a moment too soon, for in about seven seconds the balcony was jammed with spectators, including Agrippina.

"Now what?" she demanded, seeing no blood on the furniture and Little Boots quite evidently hale and hearty.

"Nero," said Little Boots.

"He didn't do anything to Little Boots," I said. "Really he didn't."

"Shut up, slave!" said Agrippina. "I didn't ask you. Learn your place, if you do not wish to be flogged." It was once more further borne in upon my consciousness that Agrippina was not fond of me.

"What did Nero do to you, Caligula?" she insisted. "Tell Mamma."

"He beat me over the head with a big stick and was going to stab me with a dagger—my brother whom I so love!" said Little Boots, sorrowfully.

Agrippina whirled on me. "Why didn't you protect my baby—you—you—you——"

"Filthy barbarian," I suggested, to help her out.

Agrippina choked; she was gathering strength for another burst when a man's voice, from the doorway, said, "What is all this commotion?" and Germanicus strode into the room. He walked over to Little Boots and examined his head, looking for cuts, bruises, and abrasions, I imagine; but of course he didn't find any. "Did Nero strike him, or threaten to stab him, Britannicus?" he asked.

I glanced fearfully at Agrippina and shook my head; then Germanicus turned Caligula over his knee and spanked his bare bottom. "This," he said, "will help to remind you not to lie." Then he laid on a few more, nicely timed, and added, "And these will remind you not to scream unless you have something to scream for, like this," and he lambasted him with a few more real stingers.

I could have suggested quite a number of additional reminders, and I think that Germanicus was trying to recall some more, when Agrippina rushed up and tore Little Boots from his embrace. "You brute!" she cried. Germanicus sighed and walked out of the room. The episode was closed.

We drove to the Forum in several vehicles to witness the triumph. Germanicus, of course, had to leave earlier than the rest of us, as he was to ride in the great procession. Agrippina and Antonia rode alone in a magnificent carpentum encrusted with

gold and set with precious jewels, its interior uphol-
stered in rarest fabrics. As usual, Agrippina was
taking it big and looking down her long nose at the
poor plebs who lined the way.

The street along which the parade was to pass on
its way to the Forum was lined on both sides by the
Roman populace; they thronged the steps of public
buildings, hung from every window and balcony,
and jammed the sidewalks, where they were held
back by the city watch.

Nero Caesar, Drusus Caesar, and Caius Caesar
rode together in a four-horse carruca, behind which
were three more, less ornate, which carried the
freedmen and slaves of the family who always
accompanied it wherever it went. I rode in that
directly behind Caius, my master.

The Roman populace, the common herd, the
plebs have always aroused within me a feeling of
disgust and loathing. They are ignorant, stupid,
cruel, debased by generations of virtual mendican-
cy. From earliest times, they have arrogantly demanded and received the dole from the government.
Even as long ago as the coming of Julius Caesar into
power there had been three hundred and twenty
thousand Romans enjoying free grain at the State's
expense, possibly half the population of the city.
Now there were a great many more—a race of mean
and unscrupulous beggars, befouled by crime and
immorality. It was these who cheered Agrippina and
her degenerate brood as they passed along the

streets of Rome that day. On the slightest pretext
they might on the morrow have torn them limb
from limb. I sometimes speculate upon the future of
an Italy peopled by the descendants of such as
these. However, Agrippina was always popular with
them.

Arriving at the Forum, we took our places in the
loge of the Emperor, from which we were to review
the parade. It was the first time that I had seen
Tiberius, and I received then an impression that
never altered: here was a great man, a great general, and a great emperor. Rome was full of his
detractors, and they increased in number and viru-
lence during the remainder of his reign and long
after his death, encouraged by those nobles who
desired a return of the Republic that they might
have free rein to rob the people and the provinces,
and by the Julians who wished to succeed to the
imperial purple.

Tiberius was an extraordinarily handsome man,
at that time about fifty-eight. He was inclined to be
shy, for he was more accustomed to the camps of
legionaries than he was to the society of corrupt and
degenerate Rome. There was constraint in the meeting of Agrippina and the Emperor. He disapproved
of her and knew that she hated him. She looked
upon him with contempt, because he belonged to
the scrofulous rather than the epileptic branch of
the family. With the children, he was smiling and

gracious, and he had a pleasant word for Antonia, the widow of his brother; but between Agrippina and himself there was but a bare exchange of coolest civilities, the civilities all being upon the part of Tiberius. As usual, the old she-wolf acted like hell. She seemed old to me then, although she was only about thirty, as I was but eleven.

However, my mind was soon relieved of thoughts concerning the Julian-Claudian feud: the martial music of horns and trumpets was announcing the approach of the parade. Being only a barbarian and a slave, I didn't occupy what might have been called the choicest place in the imperial loge; and I was stretching and craning to get a glimpse of the approaching procession, when Tiberius noticed me.

"Move up, sonny," he said, "where you can see something."

I moved with alacrity. Agrippina cast a look of disgust down her long nose at Tiberius and drew the folds of her palla aside, lest it be contaminated by contact with a slave. From that moment until his death, I would gladly have died for Tiberius.

The head of the procession was now in view. It consisted of a cohort of the city watch, the organization of some seven or eight thousand soldiers which polices Rome. The duty of this cohort was to make certain that the streets were cleared for the orderly progress of the procession. Behind them came the trumpeters and horn blowers, two or three hundred strong; then followed the cavalry cohort of five hundred men, a gorgeous sight, with their plumed and burnished helmets, their leather corselets whose metal discs scintillated in the sunlight of a cloudless Roman day. Their long spears rose upright above them, a martial forest from which they never emerged, and over all, the Roman eagles which topped their ensigns. They made a brave show.

Behind them came the singers and dancers and pantomimists, depicting in song and dance the martial exploits of Germanicus; and then the chariots, hundreds upon hundreds of them, jeweled and painted and drawn by horses gorgeously caparisoned.

After these marched several cohorts of the Praetorian Guard, and then came the most fabulous chariot of all. Long before you saw it, you knew that something of great meaning and magnificence was approaching by the great cheers of the multitude that welled to a crest and moved with it like a tidal wave which always threatened to break but never did.

It was Germanicus.

We were all very excited as we saw him coming, and nudged one another and said, "Oh, look! Here comes Germanicus," just as though everyone else in the loge were blind and did not see him, too. I forgot, in my enthusiasm and excitement, that I was only a barbarian and a slave: I nudged Tiberius. I had no more than done it when I realized what I had done, and once again I saw the crucified slaves along the Via Flaminia. Even a senator does not poke an emperor of Rome with impunity.

Tiberius looked down at me and smiled; then he patted my head. I once more dedicated my life to the business of dying for Tiberius, and it has been my one regret since that I never had the opportunity.

The chariot of Germanicus stopped before the loge of the Emperor, and Germanicus descended and knelt before Tiberius, speaking a few words of loyalty and affection, to which the Emperor replied with a little speech of praise and promise; then Germanicus returned to his chariot and moved on.

It was not until then that I saw what followed in chains on foot behind his chariot: my father and my mother. Tears welled to my eyes—tears of sorrow and of pride. You should have seen them, my son. If you had, you would be as proud as I that the blood of Britons flows in your veins. Their chins were up, their bearing that of conquerors rather than the conquered. They looked neither to the right nor to the left. It was as though they walked among human scum that they would not lower themselves to look upon. They did not even deign to glance at an emperor of Rome. The great mustachios of my father bristled belligerently. And so they passed on. I never saw them again, and it was long before I knew what became of them—after I became better acquainted with the ways of the Romans.

Behind them came a long procession of unkempt, hairy creatures who wore their chains with gutteral grumbling and with no nobility of bearing. Their hair, red-stained, added nothing to their appearance, nor did their continual scratching. These were the Germans.

Following these were a whole legion of veterans who had served under Germanicus—one of the legions that his stupidity had not lost—the proud Roman cohorts that had captured a couple of mud villages, mutinied, sought to overthrow the Emperor, and demanded largess from the public treasury. Well, they were Romans, and I suppose Romans will always be Romans until the end of time; that is if both they and the supply of poison and daggers hold out.

But I had lost interest in the triumph of Germanicus since I had seen my father and my mother, and it was not even restored when we went on to the amphitheater of Statilius Taurus to witness the games. There were athletic contests, gladiatorial combats, and encounters between men and wild beasts. It concluded for that day with the loosing of some hundred half-starved lions and tigers upon an equal number of unarmed criminals. The Roman people were in their glory.

I was glad when we got home, and gladder still when I could stretch out in the dark on my thin mattress upon the hard, marble floor at the foot of the bed where lay my semidivine master, Caius Caesar Caligula.

Chapter IV

A.U.C. 770 [A.D. 17]

✠　　✠

LITTLE BOOTS was now five years old and his education began in earnest. Tutors were assigned him and regular hours of study designated. I saw in all this some relaxation from the constant attendance upon my little master that had so irked me. During his study hours I should be free, and I looked forward to passing as much time as possible with Tibur, whose tall tales never ceased to intrigue me. Also, I wished to wander about Rome and see the sights, but I had reckoned without Little Boots. He would have no studies unless I were present.

I could, with pleasure, have wrung his Julian neck; but now that I am older I cannot but thank his supreme selfishness which once again redounded to my great advantage, though that, of course, was not his intention. He never, voluntarily and unselfishly, did me nor any other a kindly service.

With glum mien, I sat through the interminable hours of his lessons; but I couldn't shut my ears, and I commenced to learn. Finally, I took an interest, and when I did, the tutors, who were kindly men, took an interest in me. As I was older than Little Boots, I grasped things more quickly and soon forged far ahead of him. I learned to read and write not only Latin but, in the years that followed, Greek as well.

I think that the highlight of my life was when I had learned the language of the Romans sufficiently well that I could transfer my thoughts to the wax of my tablets and read the poems of Homer and the writings of Titus Livius and the works of Marcus Tullius Cicero. A new world was opened to me—a magic world of wonder.

But life was not all study. There were other things to engage our attention. One of these occurred a few days after the triumph of Germanicus: Little Boots pushed Agrippina Minor into the pool in the peristyle. Agrippina Minor was two years old and had not yet learned to swim.

I was horrified, but Little Boots laughed uproariously. "Don't touch her!" he yelled at me as I ran forward to rescue the obnoxious creature who was always bawling. "I, Caius Caesar, command. I have never seen anyone drown."

"Go chase yourself," I advised him, as I fished

the foul brat out from among the lily pads. Then I
heard something that sounded much like the war
whoop of the German hordes, and looking up saw
Agrippina Major legging it along the balcony
toward the stairway.

Knowing that in one way or another I should be
blamed for this, and ignoring for the nonce the fact
that I was the great-grandson of Cingetorix, I beat a
hasty retreat; and when I say hasty, I mean hasty.
I was out in the street and legging it for elsewhere
in what probably would have set an all-time Olym-
pian record.

In moments of great stress or danger, it is only
natural for a child to seek the protection of a friend,
and I had only one friend in Rome: Tibur. As
Romulus and Remus found a protector in the she-
wolf, I would find one, a far more ferocious one, in
the person of the ex-gladiator. He would tell me for
the fortieth time that old, old story of which I never
tired: the bloody story of the murder he had committed. He would tell me of how he twisted the
heads from lions for the edification of the Roman
populace and a Roman emperor. He would probably
search around in the gory depths of his memory and
disinter other horrendous exploits. But, more important still, he would take me to that woman in the
city who would hide me until things quieted down
or I could make my escape and start back for
Britannia. I had no doubt but that, once out of the
city, I could travel half the length of Italy, cross the

Alps, traverse the country of the Helvetians and that of the Belgians, and cross the channel to my native land. Would that I still retained that sublime self-confidence!

However, as I turned my footsteps toward the Praetorian Camp, a bug crawled into the olive oil. It became clear to me that the first place they would look for me would be the Praetorian Camp, because that was where they had found me upon that other occasion. Had I not been the great-grandson of Cingetorix, I should have been stricken with terror; and, as it is my aim to be scrupulously veracious, I shall have to admit that I only escaped it by the slim margin of one "great." Had I been just one more generation removed from Cingetorix, I might have permitted myself the satisfaction of being wholly terror-stricken without reflecting too much dishonor upon his great name.

I now reversed my route of retreat and headed for the district of towering, grimy tenements and narrow alleys, confident that no one would look for me there.

A mass of dirty, ragged children played on the even dirtier pavement of the alley where I sought refuge. As I approached them, they began to hoot and jeer, directing their opprobrious sallies at my clean tunic and new sandals; then they began to shy things at me—bits of stone and handfuls of filth. Not to be outdone in the social amenities of the Eternal City, I shied stones and handfuls of filth back at them, scoring, I noted with considerable pride, more often than they did.

Presently a boy much larger than most of the others, a boy about my own age, or perhaps a little older, detached himself from the enemy front and made a sally. He ran up quite close to me and spit on me. Now, even when I had been spit upon by a Caesar, I had not taken it lying down, nor was I of any mind to take it lying down from this scum of a pleb. I hauled off and socked him one on the nose, from which blood instantly spurted in all directions. But the lad was game. He landed a good one on my right eye; then we went into a clinch and rolled upon the pavement.

First he was on top and then I was on top, and all the time we were lambasting each other as hard as we could. He was trying to bite my nose off, and I was bending every effort of a long line of Cingetorixes to gouge his eyes out.

Surrounding us was a howling mob of enemy first-line troops, support, and reserves; and they were all kicking me in the ribs whenever they found an opening, and when there was no opening they kicked my opponent in the ribs.

Finally, during a breathing spell, the creature who was now underneath me found tongue. "Vile slave," he managed to gasp, "how dare you lay hands on a Roman freeman!"

"Thus," I replied, and conked him again—a peach, right on his mouth.

Hostilities were immediately renewed. How long it would have gone on I do not know had not someone seized us each by the scruff of the neck and jerked us to our feet. It was a soldier of the city guard, a behemoth about the size of the Arch of Augustus. The army of the enemy now vanished.

"What do you two brats think you are doing?" demanded the Arch of Augustus.

"He struck me," explained my late opponent.

"So what?" demanded the Arch.

"I am a freeman, a citizen of Rome." This was laying it on a little thick for he was not a man and he couldn't become a citizen of Rome until he came of age.

"So what?" redemanded the Arch, who seemed to be a man of few words.

"He is a slave," said the filthy little pleb haughtily.

The Arch now took a closer look at me. "So he is," he said, having pierced the blood and filth upon my tunic to see that it was the tunic of a slave. "So he is." The fellow was tiresomely repetitious.

Suddenly he commenced to shake me until I thought all my teeth would fly out of my mouth. "What do you mean by striking a Roman?" he demanded.

"He spit on me," I explained.

"Well, why shouldn't he spit on you, slave?"

"I have just shown him why he shouldn't," I explained.

"Well, come along with me and tell that to the judge when your case comes up—if it ever does."

The Arch dragged me along the streets of Rome, sometimes by an arm, sometimes by an ear. He seemed to prefer the ear because it hurt me more. He dragged me past the frowning Tullianum, built by Servius Tullius more than five hundred years ago—and it looked it. Here Spartacus had been incarcerated; Jugurtha, the Numidian king; the conspirators of Catiline; the Vercingetorix. But at the moment I was not interested in points of historical interest.

He did not take me into the Tullianum, but to another prison nearby. The Tullianum was not reserved for little boy slaves, but for more important malefactors who were awaiting execution. Perhaps, if I lived, I should someday rate the Tullianum; and the way I felt toward Rome and Romans at that moment, and especially the things that I should have liked to have done to certain members of the imperial family, and to a big gorilla of the city watch, would undoubtedly have landed me there could I have carried my dreams to realization.

At the prison to which I was taken I was pushed into a dark, foul-smelling dungeon that was already overcrowded. It was filled with the dregs of Rome, below which no other dregs have ever sunk. They were the abysmal, bottom-most precipitation of the alchemy of crime and squalor and sordidness and vice and degeneracy. There were both men and

women there, and the women were the worse. I was
the only child. They were slave, freedman, and
freeman. There were no sanitary facilities; there
was no water for bathing or for drinking. The
miasma of ordure, sweat, and disease was so over-
powering that I thought I should be suffocated by
it. I closed my eyes and sought to recall the beloved, heather-covered moors of Britannia on a
spring morning and the familiar scents of her great
oak forests; but nothing could pierce the putrid
stink of that foul dungeon and its fouler inmates.

Besotted, hopeless, inarticulate lumps of hideous
flesh, they looked at me from dull, bleared eyes as I
was thrust into their midst. I imagine that their
brains were poisoned by the noxious vapors they
constantly inhaled, only to exhale them still more
contaminated.

They talked: profanely, obscenely. There was
mirthless laughter. It might have come from the
lower regions where the dead are. One, a great brute
of a man with matted hair and beard, spoke to me.
"What brings you here, my chick?" he demanded.
"Did you, by chance, lead the gladiators in an
uprising against the Emperor? Your black eye, your
bloody nose, your scratched face, the blood and filth
upon your tunic could have been achieved in no less
ambitious an adventure."

Those around him laughed, and another man
approached me. "I like your looks, little one," he
said. "You and I shall be great friends." He was a

loathsome fellow, half-decayed from some horrid disease.

The brute who had first spoken to me stepped between us. "Lay off the young 'un," he growled. "He belongs to me."

The other bared his teeth like a beast snarling over his kill. "Try and take him," he challenged.

The brute struck a terrific blow that sent the man reeling. He stumbled over the bodies of men and women too insensate from long starvation even to protest. He fell, but he was soon up. He charged the brute, with blood running from his nose and the corners of his mouth. He made strange sounds; they were not animal sounds, nor were they human. He leaped upon the brute; and the two fell to the stone floor, biting, kicking, scratching, gouging.

I backed into a corner, horror-stricken. I had seen men battle before and I had seen men die, but they had been brave men fighting in the open—warriors of Britannia, soldiers of Rome. They fought like men, not like unclean beasts. I wondered why they fought so because of me. I was young then. I did not know, but I had a presentiment that something terrible might happen to me no matter which one was victorious.

At last the brute arose. The other lay very quiet. He did not speak nor move; he would never speak nor move again. He was dead. A woman laughed. "Served him right," she said, "but 'twere a pity that you did not die, too." The brute glowered at her.

A guard came, tardily. "What's going on in here?" he demanded. No one replied. He looked about and saw the man lying in a pool of blood. He kicked him: then he rolled him over on his back and saw that he was dead. "Who did this?" he asked. No one replied. The guard looked at the brute and saw blood on his face and his beard and his hands. "So it is you again?" he barked. "Come along with me," and he gave the brute a push toward the doorway. "We have ways of curing the likes of you of bad habits."

They went out, and the guard closed and locked the door again. "It is a good thing for you, lad," said the woman who had laughed, "that those two are out of the way. There are others here almost as bad; but they will be good for a while after this. If anyone bothers you, yell for the guard—he may come and he may not. And if he does come, he may beat you. But these others will leave you alone."

"Shut up, you filth," growled a man. "The kid is only a slave; those two were citizens of Rome—and so am I," he added.

"What did you do to get in here?" the woman asked me.

"A boy spit on me, and we fought in the street," I replied. "He was the son of a citizen; I am but a slave."

"You may die for that," said a man, "or they may send you to the mines for life."

"Would they crucify me?" I asked.

"Very probably: that is the death for slaves. It is very painful. Sometimes they live for days, screaming until their tongues swell so from thirst that they can no longer scream."

Had I a razor or a dull knife, or even a piece of glass, I should have opened my veins then and there. I did not fear to die. From earliest childhood we Britons are taught not to fear death. But crucifixion! To have spikes driven through my hands and feet, and to hang thus on a cross for days! For a moment, I was weak and sick, and then I remembered that I was the great-grandson of Cingetorix. From that moment I started schooling myself in a determination not to cry out even once, no matter how much it hurt. The shade of Cingetorix would look down upon me and be proud.

My sad thoughts were presently interrupted by the sound of dull blows, followed by screams. "He is getting what-for," said the woman, laughing. The sound of the blows continued; the sound of the screams increased. The woman counted out loud. She was counting the blows. After fifty, the screams diminished in volume; after a hundred, they ceased. "He couldn't take it," said the woman.

"They have stopped beating him," I said. "Listen! He has stopped screaming."

"The guards do not beat a corpse," said the woman, "nor does a corpse scream."

"You mean that they have beaten him to death?" She nodded.

I felt very depressed, but not because of the death of the brute. Everything here was depressing, and the future looked as black as the depths of a German forest at night.

Presently another guard came to our dungeon. "Where is the brat who was brought in here a little while ago?" he demanded.

As no one else spoke, I said, "Do you mean me?"

He looked all around the gloomy, sunless hole. "As you're the only brat here," he said, "I must mean you. What is your name? The baboon who brought you in forgot to register your name."

I did not answer at once. I was thinking. When I had first been arrested, I had determined not to divulge my name because that would mean that I should be returned to Agrippina, and this time she would certainly have me killed. But now the matter appeared to me in a slightly different light. If I remained here, I should be starved and abused and doubtless end up on a cross beside the Via Flaminia. If I were returned to the house of Antonia, either Germanicus or Little Boots might save me.

"Well?" demanded the guard. "Are you going to tell me your name, or shall I have to beat it out of you?"

"My name," I said, "is Britannicus Caligulae Servus."

A sudden hush fell upon the room. A slave of the imperial house is a person of importance. The slave of a Caesar is not to be treated lightly by the common herd; no, not even by a citizen of Rome.

The guard blew up like an overheated boiler. "What?" he bellowed. "If you are lying, may the gods help you."

"I am not lying."

"Then why didn't you say who you were before?"

"No one asked me."

"That fool baboon!" ejaculated the guard. I guessed that he referred to the Arch, and I mentally applauded the description.

"Come with me," said the guard. "The entire city watch and half the Praetorian Guard are searching the city for you."

When I entered the house of Antonia a half hour later the demesne was preternaturally quiet. I had been praying that Little Boots would be screaming, but he wasn't. Two centurions and a tribune of the Praetorian Guard escorted me into the atrium; a moment later Agrippina joined us. When her eyes fell on me, she voiced a cry of horrified disgust.

"Is this he?" asked the tribune.

"Where have you been and what have you been doing, you horrible little barbarian?" demanded Agrippina.

"I have been in prison," I said.

"Well, get up to Caligula's room at once and let him see you. Then throw those filthy garments away and bathe yourself. Ugh!"

In the room of Little Boots, I found Germanicus sitting staring at the child in a helpless sort of way. Little Boots sat on his bed with his eyes closed and his mouth wide open, apparently emitting noiseless screams: his body was racked by them.

When Germanicus saw me, he looked astonished; but he also looked relieved. He turned to Little Boots. "Open your eyes," he said. "Britannicus is here."

Little Boots opened his eyes, and when he saw me, he closed his mouth. But when he had had a better look at me, he opened it again, this time in wonder.

"What happened to you? Where have you been?" he croaked in an almost inaudible voice. I gathered immediately that he had yelled so long and so loud that he had practically lost it.

"I had a fight and I went to prison," I explained.

"Why did you have a fight?" he asked.

"A boy spit on me."

"I could have advised him differently," said Little Boots.

Germanicus grinned. "Why did you run away, Britannicus?" he asked.

"I was afraid that Agrippina would think that I pushed the baby into the pool and that she would have me beaten to death or crucified," I explained. "Now, I have to go and bathe and put on clean clothes," I added. "Agrippina told me to."

"Come right back and tell me about the fight," said Little Boots.

Germanicus walked out onto the balcony with me. He laid his hand very kindly upon my shoulder. "Do not run away again," he said. "Agrippina will not have you beaten to death or crucified; nor shall anyone else. I will see that no harm comes to you."

Germanicus may have been dumb, but he was a good scout.

Chapter V

✠   ✠

MUCH OF great importance to a boy of eleven had
transpired in A.U.C. 770, and there were even greater
adventures to come; but for various reasons I
shall have to skim over this and some subsequent
years. In the first place, I traveled so much and saw
so many strange and wonderful sights that the
picture of those years is rather blurred in my memory, like a mural, faded and defaced through long
years: only the highlights remain at all clear. Then,
too, I was absorbed in my studies, which continued
throughout all our peregrinations. But this loss to
posterity is chargeable mostly to that human atrocity, Little Boots.

It was my custom, after I had learned to write, to
make notes upon my wax tablets of various happen-
ings of interest and later to transfer them to papy-

rus rolls, filling in minor details and recording my
personal 'reactions to such occurrences as had been
of sufficient importance to arouse any reactions. I
was very proud of the result; I felt that I was
becoming a man of letters. But as many of my
observations related to members of the imperial
family and, therefore, were seldom complimentary,
I devised something in the nature of a code, or
crude shorthand, based on that developed by Marcus Tullius Tiro, the private secretary of Cicero,
which was known as Notae Tironianae.

No one but myself could read these notes. If
Agrippina had ever read them, I believe that not
even Germanicus and Little Boots together could
have saved me from ornamenting the Via Flaminia.

To make doubly sure, I kept my papyrus rolls
hidden; but one day, when we were voyaging from
Rome to Capri, Little Boots discovered them. When
he found that he could not read them all and that I
refused to read them to him, he threw two rolls
overboard into the Mediterranean. It took all the
self-control I possessed to restrain myself from
pitching Little Boots in after them. So this accounts
for the sketchiness of some years of these memoirs.

However, it is still of A.U.C. 770 that I am now
writing, the year which marked the turning point in
the affairs of Agrippina, granddaughter of Emperor
Augustus, and inaugurated that series of tragedies
which eventually placed Little Boots upon the
throne of Rome.

Shortly after his triumph, Germanicus was entrusted with a mission of high importance and ordered to Syria, where, as the representative of Tiberius, he would wield imperial power over all of the eastern provinces. Agrippina was delighted, since it would permit her to play the role of an empress, a role for which she considered herself divinely fitted. Nero, Drusus, and Little Boots were beside themselves with excitement at the prospect of the long voyage and dreams of adventure in the fabulous lands of the East; nor was I any less intrigued. That obnoxious creature, Agrippina Minor, was too young to have any opinion whatever on the subject; and if she had, it would doubtless have been that she could bawl just as irritatingly in the East as elsewhere.

"We're going in a big trireme," announced Little Boots. "I heard Papa say so. Perhaps we shall be attacked by pirates. My august ancestor, Caius Julius Caesar, for whom I am named, was once captured by pirates and held for a ransom of twenty silver talents; but he considered this an unworthy amount for a person of his importance and insisted upon paying them twenty-five talents."

Personally, I thought this nothing to brag about. Had one of my ancestors been such a silly ass, I should have kept pretty quiet about it. It seemed to me that twenty thousand denarii, which was, I imagine, about the value of twenty silver talents in the time of Julius, was considerably more than any

Caesar was ever worth. Were I asked to pay twenty thousand denarii for all the Romans in the world, I should feel that I had been grossly overcharged. I felt that they might be worth one sestertium a dozen as fertilizer, but I thought it best to keep this estimate to myself.

Since we had returned to Rome, Little Boots had been permitted to visit the Praetorian Camp quite often with a tutor and a retinue of slaves and freedmen, as it was a part of the policy of Agrippina to foster the affections and loyalty of the imperial troops, which had been manifested to so great an extent in the camps in Germany that the legionaries had threatened to mutiny if their idol were taken from them. It is certain that the rough soldiers idolized the little Caesar to whom they had given the name of Caligula, and Agrippina was shrewd enough to encourage this sentiment for political reasons. To the end, she always aspired to rule Rome: first, as the wife of Germanicus and later as the mother of an emperor; and the love and loyalty of the legions of Rome were a long step in that direction.

Little Boots and I, however, were not politically minded: the purpose and depths of our intrigues were to see Tibur. Fortunately for me, my young master shared my affection for the ex-gladiator; and when I reminded him that our projected journey would mean the end of our association with Tibur, he announced that he would not go to Syria.

"Don't make me laugh," I said. "If Agrippina says you are going to Syria, you are going to Syria."

"I'll yell," he threatened. "I'll yell all the way to Syria."

"That would make you hoarse," I said. "If you'd use your brains more and your mouth less, you could accomplish these things without so much noise."

"Be careful, slave!" he admonished. "Some day you may go too far. Don't forget, vile barbarian, that you address a Caesar."

"I only know that I address a spoiled brat," I said, "and if you don't lay off that 'slave' and 'vile barbarian' stuff, I'll tell Agrippina who put the frog in her bed. Now, if you'll quit calling names, I'll tell you how we can go to Syria and still see Tibur whenever we wish."

"That is silly," said Little Boots. "Nobody could see all the way from Syria to Rome, not even a Caesar."

"No, but we could take Tibur with us. All you have to do is tell Agrippina that you wish Tibur to accompany us and she'll tell Germanicus, and there you are!"

"I'm glad I thought of that," said Little Boots.

The day of our departure, filled with excitement, was one long to be remembered. We rode to the docks by the Campus Martius in such splendor as almost to rival a triumphal parade. Cavalry and cohorts of the Praetorian Guard preceded and fol-

lowed us: senators, nobles, and knights accompanied us, some in chariots, some on foot; and the
streets were lined with cheering thousands, for Germanicus and Agrippina were unquestionably the
most popular people in the entire Roman empire—a
sad commentary upon the intelligence of Romans.

The Campus Martius was jammed with humanity, its green turf trampled beneath myriad sandals.
It is a large, level, alluvial plain lying along the
banks of the Tiber and filled with theaters, baths,
temples, and monuments of great size and beauty.
The Romans seem to have an obsession for the
colossal. Perhaps, because they are undersized
themselves, it gives them a sense of vicarious grandeur to produce colossi; or it may be that thus they
felt they were creating something—a nation which
never created anything other than new means for
destroying life, but copied everything from the
Greeks, even to their gods, who were Greek gods
with Latin names.

Coming down from the Palatine Hill, our procession passed the Forum on the right; then, turning
from the Sacred Way, our route lay between the
Temple of Saturn and the Basilica Julia and thus to
the Campus Martius.

Riding in the carruca with me and several
freedmen was Tibur, whose presence there attested
the power of a Caesar, even a Caesar who was not
yet six years old, quite proving Little Boots' oft

repeated assertion that everything was in the power of a Caesar—some more of Agrippina's schooling.

This was the first time I had seen the Campus Martius, and I was impressed. Even great men from Greece and Egypt have raved over the beauty and magnificence of the buildings and monuments of the Campus Martius, so it is not strange that it filled the eyes of a little barbarian boy with wonder. I have always thought it far more magnificent than the Forum, possibly because of the vast expanse that it occupies, permitting each architectural gem to stand out alone without the distractions of near-by monuments to call attention from its beauty.

A multitude of people milled about, pressing forward eagerly to catch a glimpse of the members of the imperial family, so that it required more than two full cohorts of the Imperial Guard and the city watch to hold them in check. Never before had I seen so many people congregated, nor such diverse nationalities and clothing. There were tall, blond Gauls and swarthy Spaniards; black Ethiopians in long white garments; hairy Germans garbed in the skins of beasts; Greeks; Jews; bearded, burnoosed, dark-visaged men from the deserts of Arabia; in fact, representatives of all the races of the world that is the Roman Empire. There were Romans in short tunics belted at the waist; these were the plebs and the slaves, the latter in their distinctive white tunics. And in that great throng there were even the togas of the more prosperous, and people of nearly every nationality, women and children, as well as men. There were the hawkers and peddlers of sweets and cakes and fruit, crying their wares; and on the far outskirts of the crowd, little knots of people surrounded fakirs, jugglers, or other entertainers. It was, on the whole, a good-natured, well-behaved multitude, apparently as happy here and as well amused as though watching defenseless men being torn to pieces by wild beasts in the amphitheater.

I was so wide-eyed with wonder, bobbing my head from right to left and back again, trying to see everything at once, that Tibur's attention was attracted to me. "Never been here before, sonny?" he asked.

"Never. It's wonderful!"

"Well, that building on your left," he said, "is the Theater of Marcellus. Augustus built it about forty years ago in memory of his nephew who had died about ten years before, when he was twenty years old."

"It is beautiful," I said. "Augustus must have been very fond of him. Did you know him, Tibur?"

Tibur swore a great oath, but he laughed. "How old do you think I am, to have known a fellow who died fifty years ago?"

I had never given the matter any thought, but like most children I looked upon all adults as of tremendous age. "I don't know," I said.

Tibur pointed to a beautiful building on our

right, a portico enclosing two temples. "I might have come nearer knowing the old woman that was erected to," he said. "She's been dead only twenty-eight years. I was one year old then."

"Who was she?" I asked.

"Octavia," he replied.

"Who was Octavia?"

"Anyone could tell you were a barbarian," sniffed Tibur. "Why she was sister to the Emperor Augustus; one of her husbands was an emperor, too, for a while. He skipped out and lived with a dame named Cleopatra, over in Egypt; she was a bad lot, from all they say. My father saw her when she came to Rome. He said she wasn't so much to look at. But she must have had something: two Caesars fell for her.

"Just back of the Portico of Octavia is the Circus Flaminius, and that building just ahead of us on the right, that's the Theater of Pompey; it seats about ten thousand people."

The theater itself was a beautiful building of stone, marble, and stucco. Clustered about it were temples, a portico, and a large hall where the Senate used to meet.

"That's where Julius Caesar was murdered," said Tibur. "Way off to the north there, do you see that big mound and statue beyond the baths of Agrippa?"

I told him that I did. It was a huge, conical mound of earth covered with evergreen trees and surmounting a base of sculptured marble. Upon its summit towered the statue of a man.

"That's the mausoleum of Augustus," explained Tibur. "That statue of the old boy is two hundred and twenty feet above the ground. In the base is a huge sepulchral chamber where his ashes lie and fourteen smaller chambers for the members of his family."

"A lot of building just for ashes," I commented. "Think of all the money and labor they spent on that."

Tibur looked at me in surprise. "That's a funny idea," he said, and scratched his head as though he was giving the matter thought.

But now we had arrived at the dock, where a great trireme was tied up; and I was from that moment all eyes for the vessel that was to be my home for three long weeks. I had never seen so large a ship, and it did not seem possible to me that such a monster could float upon the water or that oars or sails could ever propel it to far-away Syria.

Boylike, I wanted to be all over the great ship the moment we came aboard, nor was it long before I had been into all parts of it from the benches of the galley slaves to the top of the tower on the foredeck from which the soldiers threw their weapons at the enemy in time of war, for this was a warship upon which we were to travel.

When we came aboard, the officers and men in full uniform and panoply were standing at attention

and the imperial ensign was hoisted to the mast-
head. The two great square sails were furled then,
but even so the ship made a brave show, painted in
gay colors, its bronze beak gilded and above that
the ivory embossed figurehead that was an image of
its protecting deity.

After I had peeked into every room that was not
locked and wondered at the magnificence of the
ship, I came on deck again; and there I discovered
Tibur leaning on the rail on the river side.

"What a wonderful ship!" I said to him.

"It is a good warship," he said, "but only a hulk
compared with some others. I'll wager that Agrippina will grouse because it is not large or magnificent enough to suit her. She would wish such a
ship as they say that Hiero, the tyrant of Syracuse,
had built for him in ancient times."

"But how could a ship be more wonderful than
this?" I demanded.

Tibur snorted deprecatingly. "It is but a rowboat
by comparison. Why that ship of Hiero's had twenty banks of oars and three entrances. On each side
of the middle entrance were thirty apartments for
the men, each apartment provided with four
couches. The supper room of the sailors was large
enough for fifteen couches and had within it three
chambers, each containing couches. All of these
rooms had floors of mosaic work with all sorts of
tessellated stones on which the entire story of the

Iliad was depicted in a marvelous manner. Along the upper passageways was a gymnasium and also corridors with their appointments in all respects corresponding to the magnitude of the vessel. There were many gardens, containing all kinds of plants and shaded by roofs of lead or tile. There were also tents roofed with boughs of white ivy and vines, their roots in casks filled with earth. Close by these was a temple devoted to Venus, with three couches and a floor of agate and other beautiful stones of every sort that could be found in Sicily.

"There was also a drawing room with five couches and a book case; and a bathroom large enough for three couches, all of Tauromenian marble. There were many rooms for the soldiers and for the men who manned the pumps; and in addition to all that I have told you, there were on each side stalls for ten horses with rooms for the fodder of the horses, their harness, and the arms and furnishings of the horsemen and attendants.

"Near the bow of the ship was a cistern containing two thousand measures of drinking water; and adjoining this a large pool filled with seawater, in which were great numbers of fish.

"That, sonny, was a ship."

I thought that Tibur was lying, but years later I read a similar description of the famous ship of Hiero I, Tyrant of Syracuse, and knew that Tibur was only repeating someone else's lie.

As I stood there by the rail of the trireme, listening to Tibur, my eyes devoured the beautiful panorama of hills upon the farther side of the river; and then they fell to the yellow flood of the Tiber, rolling and twisting down to the sea like something unclean—some noisome, devouring snake, sinuous, silent, all-powerful, typifying the cruel empire of Rome that reached out to gather the whole world within its coils.

Just then, moving slowly past me on the flood, I saw a naked human corpse, floating bottom up. "Look!" I cried to Tibur, and pointed.

"Some poor devil, strangled and thrown down the Gemonian steps to be hooked and dragged to the Tiber," he said.

"Why?" I asked.

Tibur shrugged. "Some criminal, perhaps," he said, "or possibly one who was thought to have designs upon the Emperor. I doubt that it was a barbarian prisoner, as there has been no triumph since that of Germanicus."

My heart stood still and I went suddenly cold. "Do they thus to those who follow in chains behind the chariot of the victor?" I asked through dry lips and a cleaving tongue.

Tibur nodded. Now I knew what had become of my father and mother, and hatred of Rome and the Caesars surged through me—a great wave of bitterness that has never receded. I turned and walked

away. I wanted to be alone; and, alone, I then
dedicated my life to one purpose—vengeance:
someday I would kill a Caesar.

Chapter VI

✠ ✠

WE FLOATED down the Tiber, the rowers plying their oars but just sufficiently to give the ship steerageway, and then through the harbor at Ostia and out upon the blue Mediterranean. Here the two great, gorgeous sails were hoisted—square sails of an ivory color, bordered all around with a band of purple which carried a design; and almost the full width of each sail, a huge Roman eagle in purple. We must have been a gorgeous sight from a little distance, the sails bellying to the breeze, the three banks of great oars moving in perfect unison, the sunlight streaming down from a cloudless sky upon the metal and ivory and the gay colors of the hull, with our pennants and ensign streaming in the wind. It was a most auspicious beginning of a journey that was to end in tragedy.

Everyone was gay and happy, even Agrippina. Germanicus, as usual, was kind to everybody. I did not wonder that people loved him. If he had only had a little more common sense! Already he was making plans, which in themselves were innocent enough, that were to further try the patience of Tiberius and fortify his convictions that Germanicus was to prove as little trustworthy a statesman as he had been a general.

Instead of sailing directly and with all speed to his post, he stopped at the islands of Sicily and Crete for the purpose of sight-seeing, and then sailed on to Alexandria, which we reached after a protracted voyage of three weeks.

In Egypt, we went up the Nile, visiting temples, tombs, the pyramids, and the Sphinx, which appeared to be a great lion with a human head.

Germanicus was in his glory but Agrippina was grumbling again, for during our stop at Syracuse on the island of Sicily the first cloud had appeared upon the horizon of that strange peace that was far too marvelous to be true. Word had come to Syracuse that Tiberius had recalled Silanus from Syria and appointed Cnaeus Piso governor in his stead.

"He has set Piso to spy upon you," I heard Agrippina say to Germanicus.

"I think Tiberius wished only to give me an experienced administrator to work with me and share the responsibility," replied Germanicus.

"Bosh!" exclaimed Agrippina. "Piso never

worked with anybody; he is arrogant and self-. willed, and his wife hates me. Mark my words, Tiberius is plotting your ruin. Don't be a fool. Get rid of the man."

When they all finally got together in Syria, after Germanicus' sight-seeing trip had been cut short by a curt message of advice from the Emperor, Agrippina's strictures, insofar as they had applied to Piso and Plancina, appeared warranted. Piso was a bull-headed, egotistical ass, and Plancina, a spiteful, jealous, troublemaker. Tiberius had made a fatal error.

Late in 771, another daughter was born to Agrippina. This rather cramped Agrippina's style for a few weeks, but she soon bounced back into the battle in full war paint.

The new baby was named Julia Livilla. Why they should wish to perpetuate the name of a couple of family adulteresses was quite beyond my barbarian mind. It seemed a scurvy trick to play on an innocent infant who was probably doomed anyway to grow up to be an insane nymphomaniac without being branded at birth. As a matter of fact, after having been banished with her sister Agrippina Minor for plotting against Caligula after he came to the throne, her death was brought about by Messalina, wife of Claudius, the emperor who succeeded Caligula, in the same year that Caligula died.

It is interesting to note that Messalina, one of the most notorious adulteresses of all time, should have caused Julia's destruction on the ground of adultery!

How proudly will future Romans be able to point to their heritage! Epilepsy, insanity, scrofula, adultery, murder, and incest will be their inalienable, imperial legacies.

The quarrel between Germanicus and Piso, fomented and fanned to white heat by Agrippina and Plancina, came to a head at Antioch, the capital of Syria, in 772, at which time Germanicus commanded Piso to leave the province; and shortly after, the latter set sail for Rome.

Almost immediately thereafter, Germanicus was taken ill and died. I think that from that moment Agrippina's latent insanity became the sole activating agent of her life.

"He was poisoned," she cried. "It is the work of Piso and Plancina, acting as the agents of Tiberius."

Her loud accusations were those of a madwoman, for which an emperor less tolerant than Tiberius would have had her destroyed. She caused the body of Germanicus to be exposed naked in a public place to prove, by certain discolorations upon the body, that he had been poisoned; and, though no such proof developed, she clung to her morbid theory.

I shall pass over the harrowing experience of the long journey back to Rome, during which we passed the ship bearing Piso back to Syria. Were I a

Roman, I should still blush at the memory of the moments during which the two ships passed close to one another, when the principals aboard them screamed insults and accusations at one another. But I thank the gods that I am a barbarian and so feel no responsibility for the acts of Romans.

I have digressed somewhat from the story of Little Boots, because the occurrences I have narrated bear directly upon his life and certainly at that time had a definite bearing upon his future, since the death of his father removed one more obstacle from his path toward the throne. It also certainly shed a light upon his character, he manifested absolutely no sorrow, and I really believe that Nero Caesar was pleased. Agrippina was heartbroken, for I am sure that she sincerely loved her husband—the one and only redeeming feature she possessed for me. In this grief, Agrippina and I for once agreed: I had lost a friend for whom I entertained real affection.

For ten years we lived in Rome at the house of Agrippina, where Little Boots and I pursued our studies. Here, there was a fine library where I had access to the works of such men as Cicero (I doubt that Agrippina knew that his writings were there), the poet Quintus Horatius Flaccus, and the historian Titus Livius. I also read in the Greek, the works of the philosopher Aristotle, the poet Homer, whose *Iliad* and *Odyssey* prompted me to become a poet (which I never did), the dramas of Aristophanes

and Euripides, which determined me to be a dram-
atist (with identical results); but that which gave
me the greatest pleasure of all was a study of the
amazing works of Euclid, the great Greek geometri-
cian. I think that these were among the happiest
days that I ever spent in Rome.

Tibur was with us. The Emperor had had a detail
from the Imperial Guard stationed at the house as a
protection for Agrippina and her children (she insisted that they were there to spy on her and,
perhaps, murder her), and Tibur was one of their
number. His special duty was to watch over Little
Boots, so he accompanied us wherever we went.

When Little Boots was about ten he developed a
passion for witnessing the bloody contests in the
arena. No games were given that did not see Little
Boots, Tibur, and me in the imperial loge, which we
usually had pretty much to ourselves, as Tiberius
loathed these spectacles and Agrippina seldom went
anywhere. Nero and Drusus were occasionally present, and often Claudius, their uncle came.

Claudius was a funny old duffer, something of a
literary dilettante. He was inclined to make very
poor jokes and laugh at them himself. Agrippina
and her followers thought him stupid and made all
kinds of fun of him, but possibly their ultimate
contempt for him was due to the fact that he was
only scrofulous instead of epileptic. Even Tiberius
evidently considered him not entirely all there, as
he studiously ignored him. All of this was to Claudi-

us' advantage, as it postulated an inherent harm-lessness which invited neither poison nor dagger. I think he wore it consciously as a buckler against these two decimators of the imperial family—and he had the last laugh, for they all died violent deaths; and Tiberius Claudius Drusus Nero Germanicus became emperor of Rome, he and all his names.

I always liked the old fellow (he was only a little over thirty at this time, but he seemed old to me; and, perhaps, now that I am writing this, I think of him more in his later years, after he became emperor). He was simple and kindly; he called me neither slave nor barbarian, but treated me for what I was: an eager, intelligent boy.

Sometimes at the games, Tibur would become so excited that it was with difficulty that he was persuaded not to jump down into the arena and show some inept contestant how most expeditiously to slay a lion or a fellow gladiator, and at such times his great bull's bellow would thunder out through the amphitheater like the voice of Jupiter Tonans as he voiced his execrations or advice.

The audiences loved it and came to expect it, and the cheers that rang out for Tibur often drowned those intended for a victor. They watched Tibur's thumb, too, and when it pointed up, theirs pointed up, and when it pointed down, down went theirs and some poor devil received the death thrust.

Sometimes, too, Drusus, the son of Tiberius, at-

tended the games with his wife, Livilla, the sister of
Germanicus; and there was often with them a man
whom I greatly detested because we slaves often
heard many things of which the general public, or
even the Emperor, was not aware. This Lucius
Aelius Sejanus was a suave sycophant who was
rapidly worming his way into the good graces of the
Emperor, and was, as we slaves knew, seeking to
alienate the affections of Livilla.

I am forced to accord this reptile mention in
these memoirs, though his name befouls the papyrus
upon which it is written, because more than any
other, perhaps, he paved the way for Caligula's
ascension of the throne—paved it with the corpses
of those he struck down by intrigue and suborna-
tion. The bloody highway that stretched from his
evil mind to the throne of Rome was not intended
for the feet of Little Boots but for those of Sejanus,
and I am confident that it was only the death of this
man that saved Caligula from the fate of the others
who stood in the path of the fellow's ambition.

During these years we were often in the palace of
Tiberius, who took considerable interest in the welfare of the children of Germanicus. The Emperor
sought in many ways to demonstrate his sympathy
for Agrippina and her family, notwithstanding the
fact that he must have known well that she was
constantly plotting against him, as nearly everybody else in Rome knew. A hundred times I have
heard her, in the presence of a mixed company of

patricians, freedmen, and even slaves, state her conviction, as though it were a proved fact, that Germanicus had been poisoned at the instigation of Tiberius and that no member of the divine Julian family was safe while he lived. Only an insane mind would have invited such risks, and only a very kindly and tolerant man would have endured her plotting and her insults for as long as did Tiberius.

It has long been the fashion in Rome to vilify Tiberius and to charge him with all manner of cruel and inhuman acts. The seeds for these slanders were sown by a madwoman and her followers and taken up and spread by those myriad minds that feed on evil reports; but I may assure you, though I hold no love for any Caesar or other Roman, that there is little or no truth in most of the infamous charges laid against him and that Tiberius was by nature a noble character and a great emperor. He was unpopular with the masses because he did not love the bloody exhibitions in the circus and would not squander enormous sums for the free entertainment of the populace, for whose edification games lasting but three or four days might drain 500,000 sestertii from the public treasury. The patricians disliked him because of his unbending pride of birth and blood and his contempt for their fawning sycophancy. A slave in an imperial household knows more of history than the historians.

I find in my notes reference to a dinner given by Tiberius in A.U.C. 775, at which occurred an incident which clearly indicated the hold that Agrippina's delusions of persecution had taken upon her warped mind. It was at a little family dinner, an informal affair at which the guests were seated at the table in chairs instead of reclining on couches, as is the foolish and uncomfortable custom of the wealthy Romans when entertaining at the evening meal.

Livia, the mother of the Emperor, was there, and Antonia, the mother of Germanicus, with Agrippina and her older children, Nero, Drusus, Caligula, and Agrippina Minor, who was then seven years old and quite as obnoxious as she had been at two when Caligula shoved her into the pool and she unfortunately failed to drown because of my ill-advised interference—an act which I have always regretted.

As usual, I stood behind Caligula. I had taken the honors from him earlier in the day by solving a problem in geometry that had stumped him completely, and just before dinner I had bested him in a game of dice, winning one hundred sestertii from him. To satisfy his spite, he made me taste every dish that was served him before he would touch it.

It was a poor joke at best and a scurvy reflection upon Tiberius. It was also extremely ill-timed, as a future occurrence quite conclusively demonstrated, but the Emperor really took it as a joke and poked fun at both Caligula and myself, telling me that he would have my statue erected in the Forum if I failed to survive the ordeal.

During the entire meal, from gustatio to tertia cena, Agrippina never once spoke. She just sat there, sullen and glowering. After Tiberius had offered the mola salsa to the household gods, the pastry, confectionery, and fruit were served; and Tiberius selected an especially choice apple and graciously handed it to Agrippina.

Without a word, she turned and passed it to a slave standing behind her chair. There was a moment of tense and terrible silence; then Tiberius turned to Livia. "Would it be any wonder," he said, "if I were to behave with severity toward one who thus publicly brands me a poisoner?"

As a social affair, the remainder of the evening was not a success.

Chapter VII

✠   ✠

By THE time I was seventeen years old, which event befell in the year 776, I felt very much a man; had I been the son of a Roman citizen, I should then have been invested with the toga virilis, the plain white garment of manhood. However, being a slave, I continued to wear the plain white tunic of a slave, nor did it seem at all probable that I should ever achieve the dignity of that heavy, uncomfortable, and ridiculous garment that even the noblest Romans laid aside with relief whenever etiquette or the caprice of an emperor permitted them to do so.

In fact, Caligula had often told me that he would never free me, and as this would have been the first step toward the possible attainment of citizenship, I felt that I had nothing to fear. I did not wish to be a citizen of Rome. I did not wish even to be a freedman. I was much better off as a slave. My only ambition along these lines was to return to Britannia and live again the happy, carefree life of a barbarian. I pined to hunt the boar and the bear, the wolf and the red deer in the oak forests of my native land, to feel again beneath my feet the reeling, swaying war chariot as it charged down upon the enemy, to smell leather and the sweat of horses and fighting men and to see blood flow in honest battle rather than in the cruel exhibitions of the amphitheater.

Caligula was now eleven and had for some time ceased to demand my constant attendance upon him, so I now occasionally had some freedom of action. This was partially due to the fact that I had forged so far ahead of him in my studies that the comparison of my recitations with his proved embarrassing to him, with the result that he imperiously forbade my attendance at his sessions with his tutors. He gave as a reason that it was beneath his dignity to share his lessons with a slave.

Taking advantage of my freedom, Agrippina often sent me upon errands. Her attitude toward me had gradually undergone a change. She had grown to tolerate me as an inescapable evil, much as might a man with the itch tolerate his affliction. The root of her animosity toward me could only have been jealousy of Caligula's dependence upon me, aggravated, perhaps, by a lack of servility upon my part which she doubtless thought ill-becoming in a slave. It did not concern her at all that I was the great-grandson of Cingetorix, but it concerned me greatly.

One afternoon she sent me upon an errand, during the execution of which I witnessed an occurrence which foreshadowed events that were to have extraordinarily evil effects upon the reign of Tiberius and the history of Rome; and upon my return home I experienced an adventure that eventually brought me the greatest happiness I have ever known in life and the most poignant sorrow.

I was to take a letter to the house of Sejanus; and that in itself was strange, as Sejanus was by now the Emperor's favorite and must, for that reason alone if for no other, have been anathema to Agrippina. What was in the letter I do not, of course, know. There is no telling what that mad brain might have conceived to write to an enemy, but I am quite sure that it was no love note. From what I saw that evening in the house of Sejanus, it may have been a warning or a threat.

Taking my time, I strolled down from the Palatine Hill, loitering before the rich shops of the jewelers, the florists, and the perfumers on the slope of the Sacred Way. The shops of the jewelers fascinated me most, for it seemed inconceivable to me that there could be enough money in all the world to purchase even a part of what was exhibited there; and I knew that there was much more within the shops that I did not see.

There were displayed the iron seal rings for men and the gold rings of the equestrian class along with a display of countless baubles designed to attract the eye of woman. There were brooches of marvelous workmanship and set with precious stones, with which the stola is fastened upon the shoulders; and there were bracelets, chains, necklaces, and earrings of such marvelous beauty as almost to take one's breath away. In the window of one shop was displayed, by favor of the Emperor, that magnificent pearl which Julius Caesar is said to have given to Servilia and for which he was reputed to have paid six million sestertii.

Still loitering, for I had no mind to return to the house of Agrippina and the company of Caligula any sooner than I had to, I entered the Forum, which is always a scene of interest and activity. I stopped before the Basilica of Julius to watch the backgammon players on the pavement of the outer colonnade. A little farther on, several men were playing at dice, though if they were playing for money there was no indication of it; and I do not think they were, as there was a member of the city watch looking on.

A beggar approached me, asking for money. He was a very old man. He carried a board on which was crudely painted a scene depicting a shipwreck. The old fellow told me that he had been a sailor on

that ship. What that had to do with his having been
reduced to beggary, he did not explain, nor why it
should entitle him to alms. I thought him a fraud,
but I gave him a copper; then I heard a crier
exhorting all and sundry to come and see a two-
headed baby. That certainly was a fraud and poorly
done: what appeared to be the mummified head of a
little monkey sewn to the neck of another monkey
mummy. As it was getting late, I passed by the
"Asiatic giant" and the "mermen" and continued on
my way toward the house of Sejanus, past groups
reading the daily news posted on a bulletin board
and others gossiping about some new scandal, arguing the respective merits of the Blue and the
Green racing stables, or just arguing. The Romans
love to hear themselves talk.

It was dusk by the time I came to the door of
Sejanus' house. A slave answered my knock and
asked me what I wished.

"I bear a letter from Agrippina for Sejanus," I
said.

He bade me enter, and then jerked his thumb in
the general direction of the peristyle. "The noble
Sejanus is there," he said.

I thought it rather lax on the part of the slave to
admit me thus and direct me to his master without
first gaining the latter's permission, but as it was
none of my business, I continued on as he had
directed. I had, of course, come to the side en-

trance, which let directly into a corridor that
opened into the peristyle.

It was not quite dark as yet, nor yet was it very
light; and as I reached the end of the corridor at
one corner of the portico which surrounded the
pool, I stopped to look about me for Sejanus. It was
well for me that I did. If I had not done so, I should
certainly not be alive today; for what I saw was
Livilla, the wife of Drusus the son of Tiberius, in
the arms of Sejanus.

They were so heatedly engaged that they did not
notice me, and I backed quickly into the darkness
of the corridor. A moment later, I found the slave
who had admitted me and handed him the letter. "I
could not find your master," I said. "You may give
him this when you see him." I breathed a sigh of
relief as I stepped out into the cool air of the
Roman night.

What I had seen filled me with sorrow for Tiberius. As for Drusus, he probably had some other
man's wife in his arms, being a dissolute and licen-
tious fellow, so I didn't waste much sympathy on
him. But poor old Tiberius! Here was the man upon
whom he was heaping honors and power, seducing
the wife of his son. But that was Rome: these were
Romans. I was, as always, proud to be a barbarian.

It was evident that I had done too much loitering, for it was now quite dark as I made my way
through the narrow streets of the city, and I had no
torch. Rome was then, as it still is, overrun by

thieves and footpads at night, men who would not
hesitate to knock one over the head or slit one's
throat for a sestertius or even less.

However, I was not afraid. I was large for my age
and correspondingly strong and agile, the two latter
attributes having been considerably developed by
the training in swordplay and boxing given me by
Tibur; and, last but not least, I am the great-
grandson of Cingetorix. Nevertheless, I kept my
eyes open; for even a great-grandson of Cingetorix
can be struck down from behind.

I was passing the mouth of a narrow alley when I
heard a scream. It was the scream of a terrified
woman, and mingled with it were the gruff voices
and oaths of men. Had I had good sense, I should
have passed on and minded my own business, but I
did nothing of the kind. Instead, I did the most
foolish thing that I possibly could have done: I ran
quickly up the alley in the direction of the cries and
presently came upon two young thugs trying to drag
a girl into a doorway.

She had stopped screaming, as one of the men
had clapped a hand over her mouth, but she strug-
gled and fought against them, and it was evidently
this that had delayed them enough so that I caught
up with them before they could get her through the
doorway.

One of the men struck her on the side of the head
just as I arrived, and almost simultaneously my fist
caught him behind an ear. He went down in a heap,

and then the other fellow threw the girl aside and came for me. This was the first opportunity I had had to put Tibur's instructions to practical use. I was sorry that he was not there to see me: he would have been very proud of me. I landed on the lout at will and pounded him into a pulp almost before you could say Jupiter Pluvius.

As soon as the fellow had released her, I had told the girl to run, and thinking that reinforcement might come to their aid at any moment in this disreputable alley, I came to the conclusion that discretion was the better part of valor and, having beaten down number two, I started to back away toward the avenue from which I had entered the alley, when I heard the girl cry out: "Quick! Behind you!" So she hadn't run, after all.

I wheeled just in time to meet number one, who had regained his feet and some of his senses and was coming for me with Roman courage: a dagger aimed at the back.

Now the proper defense for this attack had been thoroughly and sometimes painfully drilled into me by Tibur, but it was the girl's warning that saved me. To seize the fellow's wrist, twist him around and break his arm, and fell him with a blow to the jaw were things that were accomplished by Tibur's methods in not much more time than it takes to tell it.

Then I grasped the girl's hand and hustled her out of that alley. "Why didn't you run when I told you to?" I demanded, for it had frightened me a little to find her still there after I had thought that I had disposed of her two attackers, when it was entirely possible that more of their kind might come from the squalid hovels that lined both sides of the alley.

"It is a good thing for you that I didn't," she replied quite truthfully.

"I guess you're right," I said. "That fellow might easily have gotten me. It was very brave of you, and I thank you."

She said that she was the one who owed thanks. She said a number of things that made me self-conscious and uncomfortable. One would have thought, to hear her, that I had massacred an entire tribe of the Belgae single-handed.

I asked her which way she was going, and she said to the house of Helvidius Pius at the foot of the Caelian Hill; so I told her that I would accompany her all the way to the door. As you know, the Caelian Hill would be in the direction I was going, though beyond the Palatine Hill, where was the palace of Agrippina.

Although it was night, it was not dark as there was a full moon, and by its light I could see the features of my companion. She was a girl of about my own age. As a matter of fact, she was just two years younger than I, as I learned later, and she was extremely good-looking and well-formed. Her hair was very blonde, which, with her darker eyes and lashes and eyebrows, made a lovely contrast. She did not look Roman, and as I could see by her apparel that she was a slave, I judged that she was not. Of course, she might have been a Roman who had been sold into slavery by her parents as was often done, but for some reason I hoped that she was not a Roman. I knew but one Roman of whom I was really fond. That was Tibur, but I tried not to hold it against him for, after all, one has not much choice as to one's parents.

She had evidently been appraising me, though it had not been obvious, for she said, "You, too, are a slave, and you are not Roman, are you?" But then women are far more observing than men in matters that pertain to personal appearance.

"I am not Roman," I replied, rather proudly. "I am a Briton." I put a lot of pride into that statement, and it was genuine pride. "You do not look like a Roman yourself," I added.

"I am not, thank the gods," she replied. "You and I are almost neighbors. I am a Belgian."

"I have been to Belgium," I said. "I was with my father when he went with a hundred warriors to conquer the Belgae."

The girl laughed, and so did I. "Did he succeed?" she asked.

"He did not; we were taken prisoners."

"When was that?"

"In 768."

"I was seven years old then," said the girl, and

thus I learned her age: she was fifteen. "I shall never forget 768, for it was that year that I was stolen by a raiding party of Gauls and sold into slavery." Then she asked my name.

"I am called Britannicus—Britannicus Caligulae Servus."

"Oh," she exclaimed, "you are the slave of Caesar."

"Or one of them," I corrected. "The house of Agrippina is as full of Caesars as a German beard of lice—and they are about as annoying."

"You should not talk like that to strangers," she cautioned. "Do not forget that there is always the Via Flaminia for slaves," and she shuddered.

"I am not afraid to talk that way to you," I said.

"Why?" she asked.

Now that was a difficult question to answer, as there was no very practical reason why I should trust her, and I admitted it, "But," I added, "I would wager a million sestertii that you would never report me."

"Never," she said, and then she added, with a laugh, "A million sestertii! What a rich slave you must be!"

"Well," I said, "I have two hundred sestertii that I won from Caligula at dice."

Her laugh was most intoxicating: everything about her was intoxicating. I had never imagined that there could be such a girl, but of course I had not had much experience with girls. Besides that, I had based my estimation of them, and it was a very low one, on my observation of that egregious pest, Agrippina Minor, who was not eight years old and eight times as obnoxious as she had been at one.

But this girl was different; she didn't have the face of a bilious sheep and the stride of a legionary. She floated along at my side like a forest nymph, with the moonlight in her hair and life and laughter in her eyes. I wondered how anyone could have permitted her to go abroad alone in Rome at night, and so I asked her.

"My mistress sent me with a love note to a young man who lives on the Subura."

"She must be a fool," I said. "Who is she?"

"Caesonia, the daughter of Helvidius Pius."

"I should think that a woman old enough to have a lover would know better than to send a young girl out on the streets of Rome at night."

"Caesonia is very young and thoughtless, and very selfish, too. She is two years younger than I."

"You mean that a thirteen-year-old girl has a lover?" I demanded.

"Oh, yes, but then Caesonia is mature for her age and remarkably well-developed."

"But evidently not above the ears," I suggested.

The girl laughed. "The daughter of a rich senator does not have to be developed above the ears," she said.

By now we had come to the side door of the house of Helvidius Pius. The girl turned to me and held out her hand. "I thank you so much, Britannicus," she said. "That seems very meager reward for the service you did me, but what has a slave to offer?"

"Your friendship," I said.

"That you have and shall have for always."

"It is enough."

"I hope that we shall meet again," she said. "And now, good night."

I pressed her hand again and turned away, but of a sudden I remembered something and wheeled around. She had entered the house and was closing the door.

"Your name!" I cried. "I do not even know your name."

"Attica," she said, and closed the door.

Chapter VIII

✠ ✠

I DID not see Tibur for a couple of days after my encounter with the two thugs. He had gotten a few days leave and had been away on what must have been a beautiful drunk. He looked like the wrath of Jupiter Tonans the morning that he showed up for duty. The big gorilla never was much to look at, and I can assure you that a black eye and a knife wound across one cheek added nothing to his pulchritude. Besides these, his eyes were bloodshot and bleary.

When I saw him, I had to laugh. "You must have run into a Briton," I said.

"It was a door," said Tibur.

"It should be pitted against our best gladiators in the arena," I suggested.

"Shut up!" growled Tibur.

"You should have had me along to protect you,"

I taunted. "What you need is a man who can best two thugs in a dark alley—two thugs armed with daggers."

"What are you gabbing about, barbarian?" he demanded. Tibur only called me barbarian when he wished to annoy me. I am a barbarian and I am proud of it, but I don't relish being called barbarian in a certain tone of voice. The Jews are that way, too. They run around bragging about being Jews; but if anyone calls them Jew, in that tone, they get mad. "You talk as though you had bested two thugs in a dark alley—two thugs armed with daggers," he added. Then he laughed a nasty laugh.

"I did, you fungus," I said. "In an alley not far from the house of Lucius Aelius Sejanus, the evening of the day after you went away to get beaten and stabbed by a door."

Tibur's eyes opened as far as they could, which, in their present condition was not far. "In an alley not far from the house of Sejanus?" he repeated, questioningly.

"That's what I said, baboon."

"Two days ago?" he asked.

"Two days ago."

"Just what happened?" he asked. For some reason he seemed to be giving serious consideration to my story.

I told him.

"You knocked them both down; you beat one of

them up badly; you broke the arm of one. Is that what I understood you to say?"

"It is."

"In an alley near the house of Sejanus?"

"Still the same place," I assured him.

"Well, you killed one of them," he said.

"I wish I had killed them both."

"So do I," said Tibur.

"Why?" I inquired. "You don't even know what they had done."

"I know what one of them did," he said. "I came out of a house on the other side of the alley to see what the fuss was, just as the watch came hotfooting it along with the same general idea in mind; and this cuckoo that you neglected to kill told them that I had attacked them and killed his friend."

I had to laugh.

"It is no laughing matter, you blockhead," snorted Tibur. "The watch took me off to jail, and it is only because I am a member of the Imperial Guard that I am not there yet and in a good way to be thrown down the Gemonian steps or sent to the mines or the galleys for life. I may be yet. They have reported the matter to the Praefect of the Guard."

This was serious. Of course I wasn't going to let Tibur be punished for something that I had done, although I knew that it would go much harder with me than with him, Tibur being a freedman and a citizen, the latter a corollary implicit upon his membership in the Guard.

"Did the one I killed happen by any chance to be a citizen?" I asked.

Tibur nodded. "A noble Roman," he said.

That might mean the Via Flaminia for me after all. It seemed to me that the threat of that hateful road hung constantly over my head like a sword of Damocles. I saw it at that moment as though I already hung upon one of its crosses; I saw the tortured creatures struggling; I heard their groans and screams. I saw those whom death had mercifully released, and those who had hung so long that their skeletons showed through their rotted flesh. I saw the ravens and the vultures circling high, swooping low to the grisly feast, for I had been along the Via Flaminia many times.

When we rode out for pleasure, Caligula usually directed our driver to the Via Flaminia. He had two reasons: one was that he knew I loathed the place; the other that he enjoyed watching the agonies of the crucified.

"But for the compassion of Caius Caesar Caligula," he once said to me, "you might be hanging there, Britannicus. At a word from Caius Caesar Caligula, you would be. Eventually, you probably will be," and then he laughed.

"I will see that you are not punished for this," I told Tibur. "I shall go at once to the Praefect of the Guard and explain the matter."

"No, my sparrowkin," said Tibur, "you will do nothing of the sort. Probably the worst that they will do to me will be to kick me out of the Guard and send me to some lousy post in Germany: but you—that is different. You are a slave."

"But I killed the beast by accident in the protection of a girl," I argued.

Tibur shook his head. "A slave girl," he reminded me. "No matter how excellent your reason, from your point of view, the fact remains that a slave killed a Roman citizen, and that is just too damn bad for the slave."

"They shall never crucify me," I said. "I shall open my veins first."

"And wisely," said Tibur. "But you won't have to open your veins or go to the Via Flaminia, for no one shall ever know that it was you. And now let's talk of pleasanter things and borrow no more trouble. We may never hear of this matter again, the fellow that you killed was only a petty thief."

But we didn't have an opportunity to talk of pleasanter things: a slave came to summon me to Caligula. It was early, and I had hoped that my pestiferous master still slept. But no, he was awake and unusually cantankerous. As a little child, Caligula had more often been sweet and kindly than otherwise; but with each passing year I, who was always so close to him, had noticed an increasing surliness and arrogance. Year by year, he was becoming more like his divine mother. He was not constantly thus; there were times when he was quite affable, but his moods were erratic and unpredictable. This was one of his bad mornings.

"Where have you been, slave?" he demanded. "Must I, Caesar, wait all day upon the convenience of a slave, a vile barbarian? Why have you not attended me?"

"I await your commands, Caesar Pip-squeak," I said. "And, listen! Lay off that 'slave' and 'vile' stuff, or I'll knock your ears off."

At that, Caligula seemed about to explode. "I'll have you crucified!" he screamed. He appeared feverish.

"I've heard that one before," I told him. "Can't you think of something new and original?"

Words failed him. He gave me a dirty look and got out of bed and began to dress. He was mumbling and grumbling to himself all the time. "I am going to the races today," he said, as he finished dressing, "and I was going to take you with me, but now I won't."

I had wanted to go to the races very badly and had hoped that he would want to, too; but I knew my Caligula. It would never do to let him know that I had set my heart on seeing these particular races.

"That's fine," I said. "I had been hoping that I wouldn't have to go today."

"Why?" he demanded.

"Oh, I had other plans."

He looked at me narrowly for a moment and then

unloosed a nasty grin. "I shall leave for the Circus as soon as I have finished my breakfast," he said.

"Good!" I applauded.

"And you," he continued, "shall attend me. See that you are ready."

After breakfast, Caligula, Tibur, and I walked down from the Palatine Hill to the Circus Maximus and took our places in the imperial loge in the center of the side of the Circus nearest the Palatine. Already every seat was filled, other than those reserved for citizens of patrician blood or high rank, for admission was free. There were almost as many thousands milling around outside, trying to gain admittance, as there were fortunate ones who had succeeded. Among these, vendors and bookmakers circulated, calling their wares or announcing the odds, and inside there were others of their kind selling programs or cushions, confectionery and perfumes, their shrill cries rising above the babel of voices which flowed and ebbed in tumultuous waves, a sea of sound that beat as ineffectually upon the thin air as spume or spindrift on a rocky headland. But I do not have to tell you how much noise a hundred and fifty thousand Romans can make.

Caligula was busy consulting his program and picking winners, a procedure which required no great mental effort on his part, as he always placed his wagers on the Green. A bookmaker stood at his elbow recording his choices and naming the odds, which were never very favorable for the bettor who chose either the Green or the Blue, always the two favorites at this time.

The bookmaker was an obsequious, oily fellow who constantly addressed Caligula as "Caesar." He made me sick. He paid no attention to either Tibur or me, although when Caligula had finished with him, he deigned to accept our few small wagers.

Caligula leaned over and looked at my program on which I had marked my selections. I had selected the Green in some races and the Blue in others, being guided more by my knowledge of the horses and the drivers than by colors. "Who have you in the tenth race?" he asked.

"Blue," I said.

"You're crazy," announced Caligula. "The Blue hasn't a chance in that race. Look who's driving for the Green: none other than Lucius, the slave of Silvanus. He has won five hundred races, and today he is driving in the tenth race the pick of the Green stables: Spatium, Certus, Bellus, and Ferus. Take Spatium for instance, the near horse; out of Pulchra, a famous mare, by Fortis, himself the near horse in a hundred winning races. And consider Certus: a grand horse. His sire was Princeps—" and thus he went on ad nauseum. He seemed to know the performance of every horse and its ancestors back to the fourth or fifth generation. He was, when on this subject, a bore of great obnoxiousness. If he had devoted half as much time to Euclid, Aristotle, and Titus. Livius as he had to his racing forms, he would have been a savant of the first order.

Tibur caught my eye and winked. Neither of us was paying any attention to him. For my part, I was searching the stands and the loges looking for Attica.

Finally Caligula ran down like a water clock, evidently having run out of horses, although I think that some of his pedigrees reached back almost to Pegasus. Then he turned to me: "You said that you were betting on the Blue in the tenth?" he asked, with a sneer.

"Manius for the Blue looks good to me in that race," I said, "and there are no flies on his team, either. With horses like Eros, Albus, Niger, and Terror he can't lose."

"Just how good does he look to you, simpleton?" inquired Caligula.

"You are quite sure that the Green will win?" I asked.

"I know it," said Caligula. "Last night I dreamed of ten sheep in a green pasture, and yesterday Antonia's fortune-teller assured me that ten was my lucky number and green my lucky color. What more could anybody ask?"

"I would ask for horses and a driver," said Tibur. Caligula ignored the remark.

"If you are so sure of Lucius in the tenth," I suggested, "you would probably give me odds if I should lay a little wager with you."

"Absolutely," said Caligula. "Two to one."

"I have but two hundred sestertii left since I placed my other wagers. I'll bet you the two hundred against four hundred—and let Tibur hold the stakes."

"Done!" said Caligula.

Above the tumult of the crowd, we now heard the sound of fifes and trumpets. The procession that had started at the Capitol was now entering the Circus at the end to our left. The sea of voices subsided and every head was turned toward the entrance from which the musicians emerged onto the yellow sand that covered the arena. Behind these came twelve lictors bearing the fasces indicative of the authority of the official who was to preside for the day. He rode behind them in a gorgeous chariot drawn by richly caparisoned horses, his toga embroidered in gold and upon his tunic golden palm branches. In his hand he carried an ivory scepter, and over his head an attendant held a crown of gold leaf.

A ripple of applause greeted the entrance of the great man, but it swelled into a roar as the many chariots that were to compete in the races followed him onto the sand. The backers of the White, the Red, the Green, and the Blue sought to outdo one another in earsplitting volume of noise as their favorites passed in review down one side of the two-thousand-foot arena and back along the other.

The retinue in festal attire, which followed the

chariots of the contestants and the carts bearing the effigies of gods and goddesses, drawn by richly trapped horses, mules, or elephants, received their share of applause, and presently they were gone and the chariots to compete in the first race were shut in their stalls at the far end of the track.

Now, the dignitary who was aedile for the day arose in his loge and held a white cloth on high; and as he let it fall, the barriers were dropped and the four teams were off.

The first nine races held but nominal interest for me: most of my meager funds were upon Manius in the tenth. I broke a little better than even on those races.

At last the chariots were in their stalls for the tenth race, and my heart was pounding. My entire capital, barring the little I had won during the first nine races, was on the Blue. I had placed one hundred sestertii with the bookmaker at even money and two hundred against Caligula at two to one. I therefore stood to win five hundred sestertii; quite a lot of *pecunia numerate* for a seventeen-year-old slave in the household of Agrippina. Of course, as a slave, I received no wages. However, Caligula used to give me money occasionally, and I frequently won from him at dice. I also received a few coppers now and then from a couple of other slaves whom I tutored. Agrippina never gave me so much as a copper as she was as tight as the corset of an effeminate dandy. So no wonder my heart was pounding as the barriers were dropped for the tenth race.

Manius had drawn the outside position, and Lucius, the Green driver, the inside, naturally the choice position. The White and the Red were between them, the White next to the Green.

Down the opposite side of the Circus from us they raced between the long spina and the audience, the drivers, the reins tied tightly about their waists, leaning far across the fronts of their chariots, urging their horses on with shouts and whips. The wheels and the spurning hoofs scattered the yellow sand. The horses strained for the lead, the drivers for position. Manius moved slightly ahead, keeping his eyes on the three gilded goalposts where he must make his turn at the end of the spina. He was crowding the Red chariot, but its driver had no mind to be pinched off. He lashed his team, exhorting them with loud shouts, and they responded nobly. He moved up on Manius. For a moment it seemed inevitable that the two chariots would foul, and that might mean the loss of the race for both of them, perhaps death for one if he failed to draw his knife and cut the reins before he was dragged to death beneath the wheels of chariots and the hooves of the horses.

I ceased to breathe, and then Manius pulled to the right and the danger passed for the moment. Around the goalposts they swung, the first of the seven dolphins was taken down, and I breathed

again as the four chariots plunged into the straightaway on our side of the arena.

The cries, the exhortations, the advice, the curses
of the audience followed them as they rounded the
goalposts at the lower end of the arena and the first
of the seven eggs was taken down; they had completed one lap. Manius had lost distance at the first
turn, but he had made it up on the straightaway.
Now the Green, still on the inside, forged ahead
again at this second turn. It had been a close turn;
his hubcap must have grazed one of the goalposts,
for Manius, on the outside, was crowding and, in
turn, it looked as though nothing could avert a
catastrophe. But the Red held back, and now they
were off again on the other side of the spina with
Manius third from the inside instead of fourth, and
the Red trailing.

"He didn't have the guts," said Tibur.

The backers of the Red were booing and reviling
their man; others cheered on the White, the Green,
or the Blue. "Come on, Lucius!" "Good boy, Manius!" One would have thought that their throats
would have been sore after nine races, but they
were as blatantly vocal as ever.

One by one, down came the dolphins and the
eggs. Five laps had been run. The White was holding up nobly: that driver had courage. Time and
time again Manius had tried to squeeze him as he
had squeezed the Red, but the fellow would not give
an inch, and he drove superbly. I looked at my

program; the chap's name was Numerius. He was the slave of Helvidius Pius. Noting this, I looked around again for Attica, feeling sure that the family of Helvidius Pius would be present to see his horses run. As well look for a particular minnow in the sea.

They were on the sixth lap now, the next to the last. Manius was in the lead by a head but still on the outside. Numerius and Lucius were racing neck and neck. You could hear their shouts above the tumult of the crowd as they exhorted their sweat-lathered teams. The Red chariot was trailing just in the rear of the others, but slightly to their right. The driver was waiting for the chance of an accident which might pile up the other teams and let him come in the winner, and the way those three madmen were driving it was well within the range of possibility.

The leaders rounded the goals at our left in a bunch that brought the whole audience to its feet, silent and breathless; then there was a great sigh of relief as they straightened out and roared down past the imperial loge.

They were at the last turn; an attendant had his hand upon the last egg to take it down. Once again they were crowded into that hair-raising press of lunging horses, lurching chariots, and shouting men. The whips wove like venomous snakes about the backs and bodies of the frantic horses—all but the whip of Manius. During all the race he had not laid it on once. As they rounded the last goalposts,

Lucius must have let his left rein go slack, for, instead of cutting the goals close, the chariot swung out a little, striking the left wheel of the White. Manius must have seen what was coming, for he swung his team out to the right. The driver of the White laid on his whip and swerved off, but it was too late for the Green. His right wheel collapsed, the car overturned, and the four horses, the chariot, and the driver of the Red piled on top. The Red horses went down, but the terrified Green team broke away, dragging the wrecked chariot and Lucius after them; the poor devil had not had time to cut loose his reins.

Now, for an instant, the White and the Blue were racing neck and neck; then, and not until then, did Manius lay on his whip. And how that team responded! Like a spear from a catapult they shot away from the White, crossing the finish line three lengths in the lead.

The crowd roared in thunderous applause, and the terrified horses of the Green raced madly around the arena dragging the wrecked chariot and the bloody corpse of Lucius behind them.

It was a great race. As Manius drove through the Gate of Triumph with the palm of victory in his hand, Caligula arose. "Come," he said, "I am going home. I feel sick."

I was about to say I didn't wonder, when I happened to glance at his face. It was crimson. I saw that the boy had a high fever, and I kept still.

When we got home he went to bed with the measles.

That was a great day for me: I won five hundred sestertii and Caligula got the measles.

Chapter IX

✠   ✠

CALIGULA WAS a very sick boy for about two
weeks. There was a time when it seemed quite
probable that he would die. Agrippina was frantic,
and I, Britannicus, was not a little worried. What
would become of me if Caligula were to die? I had
no need to consult an oracle to know that Agrippina
would get rid of me as quickly as possible; that I
would go to the slave market seemed inevitable.
And then what?

At this time one-third of the population of Rome
were slaves, and they were not all well-treated. The
slave possessed no rights at all. His owner could do
whatever he wished with him: beat him, sell him,
kill him. For any crime he could be crucified. He
did not actually have to commit a crime in order to
meet that hideous fate; he need only be charged

with a crime. Perhaps I should come into the possession of a cruel master. I prayed that Caligula would recover.

During his illness the place was a madhouse. Constantly, sacrifices were being made to the household gods, and every day Agrippina went in person to the Temple of Venus, the tutelary goddess of the Julian clan, to make sacrifices and pray for the recovery of her son.

The palace was overrun with physicians, astrologers, soothsayers, and fortune-tellers, each of whom knew about as much what to do as the others. There was one exception: the great Roman physician, Cornelius Celsus, sent by Tiberius. He was the only one of the lot who seemed to know anything about the science of medicine or the treatment of a measles patient. When she saw him in the bedroom of Caligula, Agrippina flew into a maniacal rage and ordered him from the palace, screaming imprecations after him and accusing him of having come to poison Caligula. "As he did to the father, Tiberius would do to the son," she cried. All this was not good for the patient. But in spite of it, Caligula recovered.

While he was ill, I was not allowed in his room for fear that I might contract and carry the disease to the other children, so I had much time to myself for a couple of weeks. I never tired of exploring Rome. From the Caelian Hill to the Campus Martius, from the Tiber to the Praetorian Camp, I came to know the city almost as well as a member of the city watch, and during my jaunts I became acquainted with people as well as avenues and monuments. The one locality that I avoided was the Via Flaminia.

Many a time I loitered at some sidewalk eating place, and over my watered wine and cakes I engaged in conversation whomever chanced to wait upon me, usually another slave. But I spoke with freedmen, freemen, and patricians. Artificial social distinctions meant nothing to me. It was the man himself: his character, his intelligence, his learning that placed upon him the mark of mediocrity or superiority. I have never thought of any patrician as a patrician but only as a man. I have never thought of myself as a slave. No man is a slave unless he thinks of himself as such. No Briton can ever be a slave.

Many of the most brilliant men of Rome were nominally slaves: philosophers, poets, physicians, astronomers—usually Greek or Egyptian. In conversation with one of these I first learned of the theory that the earth is a sphere and not a flat plain as I had always supposed, and thus came to read that work of Manilius, *Astronomica*, written during the reign of Augustus. It explained many things to me. One, which had always baffled me, was that when one watched a ship sailing out to sea, it slowly disappeared from view, as though sinking beneath the waves—first the hull and last of all the masts.

I was quite excited about this and tried to expound the theory to Tibur, but he laughed at me. He was about to eat an apple at the time, and he placed a copper on top of the apple and then slowly turned the apple over. The copper fell off. "There goes that foolishness, my chick," he said. I had no answer, but I still believed that the earth was a sphere and I still so believe.

I had many acquaintances, but I had few friends. Tibur was my best. I was very fond of him, but he left much to be desired when it came to a communion of the minds. Speaking relatively, Tibur just didn't have any; and one can't commune with a vacuum. Instead of a great brain, the gods had given Tibur the muscles of a bull, the heart of a lion, and the loyalty of a dog. Being a composite of the best in beasts, he ranked right up at the top as a friend; but as a savant he was a total loss.

My wanderings about Rome were prompted largely by a hope which I endeavored to dissimulate even to myself, but one day it was realized. Whistling nonchalantly, I strolled along the foot of the Caelian Hill and out by the Via Appia toward the old rampart of Servius Tullius; and right at the Capena Gate, whom should I meet but Attica!

Although I had seen her but once before, and that at night, I recognized her even before I saw her face. I wondered if she would remember me. For some reason, which seemed most inexplicable to me at the time, my heart pounded furiously as I approached her. Could it be that the great-grandson of Cingetorix was afraid? And of a slender slave girl with golden hair!

She was talking with a young man whose face seemed familiar to me but whom I could not place. She chanced to turn as I neared her, and when she saw me her eyes lighted with recognition and pleasure. There was no mistaking it—recognition and *pleasure!* My heart leaped right up among my tonsils.

"Britannicus!" she exclaimed. She even remembered my name! I was so overcome that, for a moment, I lost the faculty of speech. Nothing like this had ever happened to me before. I had constantly conversed on easy terms with Caesars. I had even exchanged jokes with the Emperor of Rome, but the fact that a little slave girl remembered my name rendered me as inarticulate as an oyster.

And her face! Perhaps that is what stunned me to dumbness. I had thought her lovely in the uncertain light of the moon; but now that I could see her features clearly, I realized the inadequacy of the languages of the Greeks, the Romans, and the Britons.

"Attica!" I managed to croak at last. "Imagine meeting you here! You are the last person in the world I hoped to see." I was getting all mixed up and felt like a fool. What, I said to myself, is the matter with you? Had I not been such a fool, I should have known.

She turned to her companion. "This," she said by way of introduction, "is Britannicus, the young man who saved me from those two thugs. You have heard me speak of him."

"I certainly have," he said, and, I thought, with something of acerbity.

"This is Numerius, Britannicus," Attica concluded the introduction.

Now I remembered the fellow. He had driven the White chariot in the tenth race that day. He was very good-looking. I felt that he was far too good-looking. I wondered what he and Attica had been doing out here together and what they had been talking about. I began to dislike the fellow exceedingly, but I instantly realized how ridiculous was such a snap judgment.

"Oh, yes," I said. "I saw you in the tenth race the other day. You drove magnificently."

He unbent and smiled at that. "I hope you didn't have any money on me," he said.

"I shall next time. I had never seen you drive before."

"Well, don't bet on me if Manius is in the race," he advised. "There is no driver in all of Rome who can compare with Manius."

I thought that a pretty fine thing to say, and it made me change my opinion of Numerius.

"Well, I must be running along," he said. "I'm going out on the Via Appia to look at a horse for Pius. See you again, I hope. You'd better get back home, Attica, or that little she-devil will scratch your eyes out."

"I suppose he means your mistress," I said.

Attica nodded. "Yes, but Caesonia will never scratch my eyes out; I know too much about her, and she needs me, too. She wouldn't dare trust anyone else as a go-between in her affairs."

"Affairs!" I exclaimed. "You don't mean to tell me that a thirteen-year-old girl has affairs? I thought that one you told me about was just a little romantic childishness."

"You don't know Caesonia."

"I don't want to."

"I hope you never do."

How little did either of us dream how well I was to know Caesonia in years to come.

"How is your little Caesar?" asked Attica. "I understand that he has been very ill."

"He almost died. They don't know whether it was the fortune-tellers or the astrologers who saved him, but I know what it was: he's too mean to die."

Attica laughed. She had a most distractingly infectious laugh. It wrinkled her little nose and revealed a set of marvelously white and even teeth. Her eyes scintillated. I tried to think of something else to make her laugh, but she interrupted my train of thought.

"You are going out the Via Appia?" she asked.

"No," I said.

"But you were going in that direction."

I could feel the blood mounting to my face. It was just as though she *knew* why I was loitering around in this neighborhood.

"I was just walking," I explained, lamely.

She looked at me narrowly for a moment; then she laughed again. "I'll bet you were going to meet a girl," she rallied.

I got hold of myself then: the old Cingetorix assurance returned. I looked her straight in the eyes. "I hoped to," I said.

Her eyes dropped, and I saw a little flush creep into her cheeks. The score was even!

"I must be getting back home," said Attica.

"I'll walk with you; I'm going that way."

Attica nodded, and we set off slowly in the direction of the house of Helvidius Pius. For a while neither of us spoke. I was quite content. I walked in the aura of a subtle perfume that surrounded her; sometimes my arm touched hers as we walked. The sun was never brighter, the sky was never bluer, the air was never sweeter.

"This Numerius," I said. "You see a great deal of him, I suppose!"

"Oh, yes," replied Attica.

"He seems to be a very nice chap."

"He is wonderful, and such a charioteer!"

"He is very good-looking," I said.

"He is beautiful!" exclaimed Attica.

We were at the door of the house of Helvidius Pius.

"I suppose you are very fond of him," I said.

"Oh, very!" said Attica. "And now goodby; I must hurry in."

She did, and closed the door. I walked on toward the Palatine Hill and the palace of Agrippina. I thought: What an abominable day this is.

As I entered a side door, the house seemed very quiet. It was as though it were deserted. This suited my mood, and I went out into the gardens behind the palace that I might be alone and undisturbed for as long as possible.

I found Tibur there. I did not wish to talk, but Tibur did. "What ho, sonny!" he cried. "Where have you been?"

"Walking," I said, glumly.

"Where?"

"Around."

"What makes you so cross?"

"I am not cross."

"You are as cross as a bear with a javelin in his guts."

"Do you remember the fellow who drove the White chariot in the tenth race the other day?" I asked.

"Numerius? Yes. An excellent charioteer. A nice fellow, too. I know him."

"Do you think him very good-looking?"

"Very."

"Oh," I said.

"He is one of the handsomest fellows in Rome. Why did you ask?"

"Did I ask?"

"Of course you asked. What's the matter with you? Have you gone crazy? You had better go in and lie down. You must have a fever. Maybe you are coming down with measles. Caligula was cranky like that the day he came down. Don't you remember how cranky he was?"

"Listen, Cicero," I said, "I didn't come out here to listen to an oration. I came out here for quiet and peace."

Tibur scratched his head. "You weren't drunk last night, were you?"

"Of course not."

"The she-wolf was looking for you. I thought I'd tell you so that you could have a good alibi ready."

"What did she want of me?"

"She wanted you to go out and search for Nero and Drusus. They didn't come home last night. She had everybody looking for them."

"I hope they never come home," I said.

"Well, so did I; but they came home. The city watch found them sleeping off a drunk in the house of Amaryllia."

Amaryllia was the notorious keeper of a lupanar of ill fame. Nero was seventeen and Drusus but sixteen, yet they had already started upon their dissolute careers.

"I almost feel sorry for Rome," I said.

"Why?" asked Tibur.

"Nero is weak-minded and vicious by nature; dissipation will make him worse, and some day he may be emperor."

Tibur scratched his head again. "Yes," he said, "I never thought of that. Well, Drusus, Tiberius' son, is ahead of him and maybe Gemellus, the grandson. And there is even Claudius."

"Claudius is a good man," I said, "but everybody thinks him dumb; so Tiberius will never name him his successor; and Gemellus is too young. If Drusus drinks himself to death, Nero will be emperor."

"Then you will be out of luck. He doesn't like you."

"He doesn't like anybody but himself, and he can't kill everybody."

"There is nothing that a Caesar can't do," Tibur reminded me.

Just then a slave came into the garden, and behind him were four soldiers of the Praetorian Guard. "There he is," said the slave, pointing in our direction.

"Hello, Tibur!" greeted one of the soldiers. as they advanced toward us.

"Hi, Vaburu!" returned Tibur. "What are you baboons doing here?"

"We have come to arrest you, you big gorilla," explained Vaburu, "and you'd better not make us any trouble. There are four of us."

"Do you think I can't count, you fungus? Who told you to arrest me, and why? Where is your warrant?"

"Here," said Vaburu, holding out a paper.

"Read it," said Tibur, handing it to me. "My eyes hurt."

As a matter of fact, he could not read, and he was very sensitive about it. I took the warrant and read it.

"It is an order for your arrest," I said, "for the murder of one Cassiu, citizen of Rome, and it is signed by the Praefect of the Praetorian Guard."

"Will you come along now, peaceably?" demanded Vaburu.

"Of course I will," said Tibur, "but not because I have to. I could kill all four of you if I wanted to, and you know it."

"Yes, we know it; so does the Praefect. That is why he sent ten of us; the other six are waiting outside."

Tibur grinned from ear to ear. He realized that a great compliment had been paid him. He handed over his weapons and went away with them quite cheerfully.

But I was not cheerful. The day that had started

so auspiciously had become progressively more barren and gloomy. All it needed now to complete it was Agrippina.

Chapter X

✠　　✠

TIBUR WAS imprisoned in a jail near the Tullianum and not far from that in which I had been incarcerated. I went daily to visit him, bringing him presents of food and wine. He was a great man in the jail, for he had been a popular gladiator before he became a legionary. Even the guards were obsequious to him, so he fared well. So much so that he had a room to himself when he wished it.

"This is not bad at all," he told me. "I live like a senator, with no labor and no responsibility. I have servants whom I do not have to pay. The State feeds me, and you bring me wine and delicacies. Had I known that it would be like this, I should have murdered a Roman citizen long ago." And then his great, booming laugh echoed throughout the vaulted chambers of the gloomy prison.

But he couldn't fool me. I knew that he was worried. So was I. Every day I asked when the trial was to be, but no one knew. I would be at the trial; perhaps they would acquit Tibur, for he was innocent. If they didn't—

I spent sleepless nights, and when I did sleep my dreams were horrid dreams. From thinking of the tortured creatures along the Via Flaminia, I dreamed of them. Only it was I upon a cross in my dreams. Had it been the reality, I could not have suffered more. I awoke bathed in cold sweat. But it would not be! I swore it. I found a razor, and I carried it with me always, hidden beneath my tunic.

And then one day they told me at the jail that Tibur was to be tried in the Basillica of Julius in an hour's time. They would not let me see him that morning. It seemed to me that already he had been condemned to death. My poor Tibur! Great, uncouth hulk of pure gold! My one and only friend!

I was there when he was brought in. The jury filed in. The prosecutor was there. Tibur had no lawyer. I had begged Agrippina to employ one, but she had refused. "Why should I pay out money to defend a murderer, slave?" she demanded. "It will be better if he is dead. I never did like the hulking brute."

At last the Praetorian Praefect entered. It was he who was to conduct the trial. My heart sank. The fellow was a creature of Sejanus, and the mere fact that Tibur was attached to the household of Agrippina would prejudice the Praefect against him.

One after another, the prosecutor questioned witnesses; and one after another they perjured themselves. Three, who had not been in the alley at all during my encounter with the thugs, swore that they had seen the entire affair, that Tibur had picked the quarrel, that they had seen him kill the man. Each one identified Tibur as the murderer.

Not one of them had ever seen Tibur close up before that night. They did not know him, nor anything about him other than he had once been a gladiator whom some of them had seen in the arena. They could have had nothing against him personally. The only reasons in the world that they could have had for testifying at all were the inherent Roman bias for blood and torture and the common inclination of the vulgar for exhibitionism. For these brief moments in the public eye they would send an innocent man to his death—they hoped.

When they had testified, the Praefect questioned Tibur. "Why did you kill Cassiu?" he demanded.

"I did not kill Cassiu," replied Tibur. "He was dead when I first saw him."

"But you were in the alley when he was killed."

"I was not. I was in a house on the alley, and when I heard screaming and cursing, I came out to see what it was all about."

"A likely story," said the Praefect, "in view of

the testimony of these reputable citizens who saw
you commit the murder. Have you anything else to
say in your defense?"

"Only that these witnesses are all liars," said
Tibur.

The Praefect turned to the jury. "You have heard
the testimony," he said. "There can be no doubt of
the guilt of this man, a former gladiator, ruthless,
brutal, steeped in blood. A human life means nothing to such as he. Your duty is clear. I assume that,
there being no alternative, you will find him
guilty."

The jurors fidgeted on their bench and whispered
among themselves for a few moments; then they
pronounced their verdict: Guilty.

The Praefect nodded in commendation. "Tibur,"
he said, "under the Cornelian Law on Assassins I
could sentence you to death; but because of your
service to the State with the army in the provinces
and in the Imperial Guard in Rome, I shall be
lenient. I therefore sentence you to the mines for
life."

I was appalled; so was Tibur, but he took it like
a man. The injustice of it! The farcical trial! The
unquestionable prejudice of the judge! The biased
charge to the jury! The indecent haste with which
the whole affair had been conducted!

I stood up. I was filled with rage. Perhaps I
didn't realize what I was doing, but I know that

under like circumstances I should do the same again.

"So this is Roman justice!" I shouted.

The Praefect looked at me; everybody looked at me. "What is the meaning of this, fellow?" demanded the Praefect. "Who are you?"

"I am the man who killed Cassiu," I said. "Tibur is innocent; he was not even in the alley when I killed the man."

"What is your name?" demanded the Praefect.

"Britannicus Caligulae Servus."

"So!" he exclaimed. "You, a slave, admit having killed a Roman citizen?"

"I didn't intend to kill him; I didn't know that I had killed him until two days later."

"But you killed Cassiu!"

"He and his companions were attacking a girl," I explained. "I only wished to save her from them."

"Who is that girl? Why is she not here to testify?"

"She is a slave girl. I do not know why she is not here."

"A slave girl! So there were two slaves implicated in the murder of a citizen of Rome!" The fellow rolled this morsel around his tongue as one might a choice viand. It *was* a choice viand to such as he. "What is the girl's name?"

"I don't know," I replied. "She ran away the moment the honorable citizens of Rome released her."

"You don't know her? A likely story, but it is more likely that she was your accomplice. Doubtless we have uncovered here the beginning of another plot to foment an uprising of the slaves and the massacre of countless Roman citizens."

That was so funny that I had to laugh, which was unwise. It seemed to infuriate the Praefect. "So!" he exclaimed. "You laugh! A hardened criminal and plotter." He turned to the witnesses. "Do any of you recognize this man?" he asked.

"Yes," said a fellow with an arm in a sling. "I recognize him now. He is the fellow who broke my arm and killed Cassiu. It was quite dark in the alley, and at first I thought that it was Tibur who had attacked us, but now I see that I was mistaken. It was this slave."

The Praefect turned toward Tibur. "You are free, my good fellow," he said. "It is fortunate for you that we were able to apprehend the guilty man." Then he wheeled on me. "You have confessed, slave, to the murder of a Roman citizen, and your testimony has been corroborated by a reputable citizen of Rome. There is, therefore, no need for a trial. I sentence you to death—by crucifixion."

I turned cold. It was such cold as no man might know even upon the highest pinnacle of the winter Alps. It was a cold that penetrated the spirit and the soul. Crucifixion! For a moment I felt my knees give way; and then, to my rescue, came the memory of my heritage: you are the great-grandson of

Cingetorix! I stood very straight and proud and looked the Praefect in the eyes with no sign of the hideous fear that gnawed at my vitals.

"Take him to the Tullianum to await execution," the Praefect directed the chief bailiff.

The Tullianum! I recalled that other time that I had been arrested and imprisoned. The Arch of Augustus had dragged me past that dismal pile brooding over the five hundred years of human misery and hopelessness and suffering that it had held locked in its stony heart. What wails of grief, what cries of anguish its walls of hewn rock must have absorbed!

The Tullianum! The very sight of the building, the very name had always filled me with involuntary dread. Here were incarcerated only those who were condemned to die. As the chief bailiff led me through that massive doorway I looked long at it, for I knew that it was the last doorway I should enter in this life. I was entering my own sepulcher. I was already dead. My heart still beat. The red blood still flowed in my veins. Yet I was entering my grave—dead.

The Tullianum was cold and damp and clammy, although it was summer in that other world from which I had just come. Perhaps the dampness was from the five hundred years of tears that had been shed here, and the coldness from the hearts of those who sent men here.

My jailers were not unkind. They were members

of the city watch, quasi-soldiers with the psychology of soldiers: a rough and jovial lenience when not aroused to the sterner demands of their vocation. They had no desire to be either cruel or brutal. As long as I gave them no trouble, I was a boon companion to whom they told monstrous stories of their exploits with enemies, with criminals, and with women—especially with women. It is strange how men, more or less segregated, love to expound endlessly upon their conquests in the lists of love. I gave them no trouble.

One old fellow, who had been here for many years yet had never risen above the status of a common guard, endeavored to cheer me up. "Well, young fellow," he said, "you certainly placed in tough luck. There isn't any death so painful as crucifixion; no, not even burning at the stake, for that is over much sooner. Most of them that are going to be crucified don't never sleep while they are waiting in here for the day. Lots of 'em scream for hours, and some of 'em go crazy. They'd like to open their veins, but we don't let 'em have anything to do it with—like we took away that razor you had hid in your tunic. We knew what you had it there for, and though I don't say that we *wanted* to take it away from you, we just naturally *had* to. If you'd used it, some of us would have paid for it—maybe gone to the mines for a while.

"I usually go out with 'em when they are taken to the Via Flaminia. Like as not I'll go out along with you. When they first drive the spikes through your hands, that never seems to hurt so much; it's when they drive 'em through your feet that you start to scream."

"I will not scream," I said.

"Oh, yes you will, sonny. And then when they raise the cross and the drag comes on your hands and feet and tears the wounds wider! Boy! You'll scream to high heaven then."

"I will *not* scream!" I repeated.

"Oh, yes you will, sonny; and you'll keep on screaming until you are hoarse, and after a day your tongue will swell up so that you couldn't scream if you wanted to. You'll think the wounds hurt, but wait until the thirst comes. And all the time you'll be praying for death, and death won't come—not right away. But the vultures will and the ravens. If you don't keep shaking your head, they'll think you're dead and they'll go for you. They'll go for your eyes first."

The head jailer called him and he left my cell, but he promised to come back and visit me later. "I always feel sorry for you poor devils," he said, as he was leaving, "and I like to do what I can to cheer you up."

I thanked him.

A day passed, and then another. I wondered when they were going to do it. I asked the cheerful old man. "I don't know what the delay is," he said. "Sometimes there is a delay because the lawyers are appealing the sentence, but that is for rich men or nobles. You ain't got a chance for any appeal—for two reasons. The first is because you're a slave and anyway you didn't have any lawyer; and the second is that you were tried before the Praetorian Praefect, and his judgments can only be appealed to the Emperor. It ain't likely that Tiberius is going to listen to any appeal from a slave, or that anyone would have the guts to take such a trivial matter to him."

I didn't think it was trivial.

No one visited me. I thought it strange that Tibur didn't come to see me, and I mentioned this to Sunshine, as I had come to call the old guard—to myself.

"No visitors are allowed in the Tullianum," he told me. "They used to, but after a few prisoners had opened their veins with razors or bits of glass smuggled in to 'em by friends, they issued this here new order. It's too bad, too, for we used to pick up quite a few sestertii from the rich ones for furnishing them razors. We always blamed it on their visitors.

"How you feelin', sonny? Pretty low, I guess. Well, I don't blame you none. They'll probably take you out tomorrow, and when a fellow's got that to look forward to all night it don't make him feel so chipper."

At last Sunshine left me, and I lay down on the straw pallet that was my bed. For some reason I felt that this was my last night, but I determined to sleep, as I had the other nights. I made myself sleep by repeating over and over again to myself, you are the great-grandson of Cingetorix. You are not afraid.

But this, my last night, as I thought it. I let my mind rove back through the past—back to all the pleasant things in my life that I could recall. I thought of my mother. She was different from all the other women I had known as a child. She had been very young—much younger than my father—and she had been beautiful. She had been very kind. Not all the women of the Britons are kind, for we are a fierce race and kindness is often thought of as a weakness.

I recalled the battles in which I had driven the war chariot of my father. I lived again those thrilling moments when I held the nervous, plunging horses, excited by the cries and tumult of battle, and followed my father into the thick of the fight: and I felt a tingling of pride as I realized that never had I failed to have the chariot in the right place when my father's fighting men were ready to leap to the pole and run back to it between the rearing, dancing horses. Father had always been last: his great sword red with blood, his proud mustachios bristling fiercely.

I had gone into the forests with him when he hunted: those days were the pleasantest memories of my childhood. My father feared nothing on the earth or in the heavens. I think he was the bravest man I have ever known. He hunted the wild boar and the bear with sword and spear, and on foot. He never gave an inch, even in the face of the fiercest charge, and he carried scars from his scalp to his toes. He wore them with pride, as the Roman legionaries wear their medals.

But I saved my happiest memory for the last, and I fell asleep thinking of Attica. I would not allow Numerius to even enter my mind.

Chapter XI

A.U.C.776 [A.D. 23]

✠   ✠

WHEN I awoke the next morning, I lay with my eyes closed, slowly gathering together the rambling threads of consciousness. It was good to be alive. I stretched the muscles of my young body in voluptuous repose, wondering if Caligula were yet awake and what we should do with this new day. Then I opened my eyes!

Where was I? For an instant I was bewildered and confused. These bare walls of cut stone! This gloomy chamber! The truth rushed upon me like a ravening demon as full consciousness returned. I turned over and buried my face in my poor pallet, trying to shut out the hideous truth that my eyes had revealed.

O, benign sleep! Why have you deserted me? Would that I might sleep forever! But I soon shall:

that is all that I have to look forward to. It is what lies between that terrifies me.

"They shan't! They shan't!" I cried aloud. There must be some way. I bit at the vein in my wrist. I would cheat them of the pleasure of the torture. I would die thus before they could nail me to their cross.

The old guard came hurrying in. "What you yellin' about?" he demanded, and then he saw what I was trying to do. He jerked my wrist roughly from my teeth. "So, ho!" he cried. "That is the way you were trying to cheat us! Now I suppose I shall have to sit here and watch you until they come for you. I should beat you for this, but what is the use? My little beating would be but a happiness for you compared with what will soon be coming to you."

My breakfast was brought to me and I ate. I was not hungry, but I did not want them to think that I was afraid. Old Sunshine regaled me with detailed accounts of the agonies he had seen endured upon the crosses of the Via Flaminia. After about so much of a thing like that, one becomes insensitive to more. All of the terrors that he recounted could not equal those that I had already suffered in imagination.

Between the fourth and fifth hours, another guard entered my cell. "I think they are coming for you," he said. "There's a detachment of the city watch coming down the street. They would not be coming for any other purpose at this time in the morning."

I stood up. I stood very straight, as my father had stood before the Emperor that day in the Forum.

"I'd hate to be in your boots," said the guard. "I'd certainly be scared stiff."

"I am not afraid," I said.

He eyed me intently for a moment, and then he shook his head. "May Jupiter blast me! you don't look afraid, but maybe you don't understand just what they are going to do to you."

"Old Sunshine, here, has been giving me all the details for the past two days—not omitting the ravens and the vultures."

" 'Old Sunshine'!" The fellow laughed uproariously.

Just then the chief jailer came down the corridor followed by a detachment of the city watch. He swung open the door and they entered. Behind them were two slaves carrying a great wooden cross.

"Help him get it on his back," said the chief jailer to the two slaves. "Walk beside him; he may need a little help—the cross is heavy." He turned to me. "I'm sorry for you, my boy," he said. He must have been a decent sort of fellow at heart.

The men of the city watch surrounded me, and we marched from the Tullianum out into the streets of Rome. Sunshine, true to his prediction, accompanied me. He carried some spikes and a heavy hammer.

"I'm going to nail you on," he announced cheerfully. "I'll try not to miss the head of the spikes too often."

"That is kind of you," I said.

The cross was heavy. I had to walk bent almost doubled beneath it. Some street urchins tagged along with us. They shouted gibes and taunts at me. They did not know me. They did not know what I had done. They would have thrown stones at me had not the city watch threatened them. Theirs was the inborn, primitive cruelty of children. The men who guarded me were not unkind. They seemed genuinely sorry for me. I have found that soldiers are usually neither so bloodthirsty nor cruel as civilians.

Presently some women joined the procession. They laughed and talked and gossiped and seemed to be deriving much anticipatory pleasure from the show they were about to witness: they might have been on their way to the theater to see a comedy enacted. Soon there were fully a hundred spectators marching with us—men, women, and children—and the crowd was constantly being augmented by new recruits. All the world loves a free show.

The cross was very heavy. I tried hard not to stagger, but I could not help it. Then the slaves took hold of it and helped me. They had kind hearts. Perhaps they were thinking that some day they might be carrying such a cross out to the Via Flaminia.

I thought that that march of death would never end. I wanted it to end. I wanted to get the whole horrible thing over with. Over and over I swore to myself that I would make no outcry. I would show them how the great-grandson of Cingetorix could die. No matter how much it hurt, I would make no sound. I would not give the Roman mob that satisfaction.

At last we were outside the city on the Via Flaminia, and presently we came to the place beside the road where I was to be crucified. They told me to throw down the cross; then four members of the watch took hold of me to throw me down upon it.

I shook them off. "I will lie down myself," I said. "You will not have to hold me down."

One of them slapped me on the back. "Good luck!" he said.

I lay down upon the cross. I felt the rough, unsmoothed surface against my back. I stretched my arms out along the crossbeam. Sunshine knelt beside me. In the distance I could hear someone shouting. Sunshine was placing the point of a spike against the palm of my right hand. The shouting sounded closer and closer. Sunshine's old fingers fumbled the spike and it dropped into the grass. He swore lustily and pawed around searching for it.

"Don't worry, sonny," he said, encouragingly, "I'll have you nailed on in no time at all, just as soon as I can find this damned spike."

The crowd was pressing in all around us, only

kept from trampling on us by the guard. The people were poking fun at Sunshine. "Hurry, old greasy-fingers," shouted someone. "How much longer do you think we're going to wait for the show?"

Now the shouting that I heard was much louder and closer. It had risen to a bellow. Sunshine had recovered the spike. "Now, sonny," he said, "I'll have you spiked on in no time. You said you wouldn't scream, but you will, sonny. All ready now!"

He placed the spike again and raised the hammer, and just then something struck that crowd from the rear that burst it wide asunder as though a wild bull had hit it. Even the members of the city watch were hurled aside, and a giant hand seized Sunshine and tossed him a good fifteen feet to one side. It was Tibur!

The city watch came for him with drawn swords, but he waved them off with a sheet of parchment. "A pardon!" he gasped breathlessly. "A pardon from the Emperor."

The officer in charge read it and then helped me to my feet. "You're in luck, sonny," he said. "You're a free man."

Tibur looked haggard, but he was smiling. "That was a close call, my boy," he said.

"How did it happen?" I asked.

"It is quite a long story," he said, "but I'll make it short and tell you about it as we walk home. First, I went to Agrippina and asked her to try to

save you. I was sure that if she asked, it would be
granted; but the old she-wolf just laughed at me.
'Good riddance,' she said. 'I am glad to have seen
the last of that nasty little barbarian.'

" 'But Caligula!' I reminded her. 'He is very
fond of Britannicus. He will be very angry '

" 'It's time he got over being fond of the slave,'
she said. 'He hasn't seen him for two weeks now; so
he's used to it. It couldn't have happened at a better
time.'

" 'But——' I started.

" 'Enough!' she snapped. 'I wish never to hear
his name mentioned again. You may go.'

"Then I tried to see Caligula, but she must have
anticipated something like that, for the guard at the
door wouldn't let me near him. After that I spent
two days trying to get an audience with the Emper-
or, and I only just succeeded this morning. I told
him the whole story, and when I had finished, he
called a secretary and dictated the pardon. He
didn't hesitate a moment.

"After he had signed it, he handed it to me and
smiled. 'There,' he said; 'I cannot permit them to
crucify one of my friends. I have not too many at
best.'

"I started on a run for the Tullianum; and it is
well that I ran, for when I got there, they told me
that you had already been taken out; then I ran all
the way out the Via Flaminia until I found you."

When I think of Germanicus and Tiberius and

Tibur, I am often ashamed of myself that I hate the Romans so. They are not all bad. It has just been my misfortune to have been thrown among some of the worst of them. The fawning nobles and senators, whom Tiberius held in contempt, as he did all sycophants, accused him of being haughty and arrogant; yet he could be kind and even friendly to a slave boy. Tibur, a brutal gladiator, who would as gladly have killed a man as he would a cockroach, was, toward me, always gentle and sympathetic; and Germanicus, during the little more than two years that I knew him before his death, always treated me with great kindness. I have known other fine Romans, but these three were outstanding.

When Tibur and I arrived at the palace of Agrippina and the old girl saw me, I thought that she was going to throw a fit. "You back?" she shouted at me. "I thought they were going to crucify you. If you have escaped from the Tullianum, you needn't think that you are going to hide yourself here, for I shall send you right back."

"I did not escape from the Tullianum," I said. "The Emperor pardoned me."

The cords on her long neck stood out and she turned almost purple in the face. I thought that she was going to burst out into one of her tirades, but she only grunted, "Hmm!" and said, "He would!" You would have been surprised at how much violence and viciousness a person could compress into those two little words.

The following day, Caligula was allowed to come from his room, and the regular routine of my life was resumed. He was much interested in the account of my fight in the alley, my trial and sentence, and my imprisonment in the Tullianum, and he had the grace to say that he was glad that I had not been crucified.

"That Praefect had a lot of nerve," he commented, "sentencing the slave of a Caesar to death. If you are ever crucified, it will be I who order it."

"That will make it much nicer," I said.

Although I no longer studied or recited with Caligula, I kept up my studies, and the tutors often helped me in their spare time. I was particularly interested in mathematics, engineering, and military science. I could speak, read, and write Latin and Greek, and I had a working knowledge of Egyptian. I had almost forgotten my native language, but it would have been of little use to me. All of the great and important works were in Latin or Greek. My little island had as yet no literature; maybe it will never have any. Perhaps it will be as well, if culture produces such creatures as the Romans.

The Roman patrician is haughty, arrogant, and heartless to those of lesser blood, unless they have great wealth, and a fawning sycophant in the presence of the emperor. The knights are avaricious money-grubbers, usurers, and worse. They are notoriously dishonest. The common people, the plebs, are a race of undisciplined beggars, degraded by generations of public charity: the dole has reduced them to the status of whining, snarling mendicants. They are without loyalty or courage or honor, and they are rotten with vice and crime.

I pray that Roman civilization never comes to Britannia.

As you may imagine, about everything that happened in Rome was known to the slaves in an imperial household, often before it was known to their masters, and our household was no exception. Just at the moment of which I am writing, the affair of Sejanus and Livilla was the favorite meat of the gossipers. They chewed upon it and rolled it about their tongues as the choicest of morsels. How they would have pricked up their ears and licked their chops had I told them what I had seen. But I didn't. I won't deny that I listened to gossip, but I didn't indulge in it. I might gossip with Tibur occasionally but not with the others, and of this matter I did not even speak to him. I cannot explain exactly why, but somehow I felt that it would be disloyal to Tiberius. Then, too, I had sense enough to realize that a slave who had too much knowledge and revealed it, might be thought to have too much for the good of his health. Perhaps the Via Flaminia influenced me.

The family was at dinner one evening a couple of weeks after my release from the Tullianum. I was, as usual, standing behind Caligula, where I was compelled to listen to the usual family wrangling without being able to choke any of them. Agrippina had been lecturing Nero on his dissolute conduct, and he was sitting sullen and morose. Drusus Caesar egged her on, although he was just as vicious as his brother.

"You needn't talk," said Agrippina Minor. "I heard you come in this morning, and I saw you, too."

"Shut your mouth, fungus," growled Drusus Caesar.

"Yah!" countered Agrippina Minor, and stuck out her tongue at him.

"Children!" snapped Agrippina.

Caligula, who was sitting next to the eight-year-old horror, pricked her leg with a fork, whereupon she slapped his face and began to bawl. It was a pretty scene of domestic felicity, but one to which I was thoroughly accustomed.

"These brats," said Nero, "should not be allowed to come to the table until they know how to behave. They should eat with the slaves."

"That," said Caligula, "would be preferable to eating with a conceited ass who smells of brothels."

Nero seized a large silver saltcellar and threw it at Caligula's head. It missed and hit Agrippina Minor, unfortunately but a glancing blow. Nero was but demonstrating that total abandonment of discretion which seems to be an outstanding characteristic of the epileptic branch of the imperial family.

"Children!" This time Agrippina stood up and screamed it, and it had the desired effect. The surly brood returned to the business of fortifying themselves for future family pleasantries. They now ate in silence, but their eyes and facial muscles bespoke eloquently their mutual loathing. All but Drusilla. She was by far the best of them, but she was only six and might outgrow it.

Following the main part of the meal, Agrippina arose and offered the mola salsa to the household gods. I wondered what they thought of those who were propitiating them, but as they were the spirits of the family ancestors, they doubtless took some of the burden of responsibility on their own shoulders and merely said, "Ho hum!"

During the dessert, a freedman entered and whispered something to Agrippina. I thought that it must be good news, for her face lighted up, and she looked almost pleasant. It crossed my mind that something unpleasant must have happened to someone. I was right.

"Children," she said, "the Emperor's son, Nero Claudius Drusus Caesar, is dead."

Nero made no effort to conceal his elation: another obstacle had been removed from his path to the throne—and from the path of Caligula, too; but no one gave any thought to that, unless it might have been Caligula himself.

"You forget Tiberius Gemellus," he said.

"He is only four," snapped Agrippina, "and something might happen to him."

"Something might happen to Nero," said Drusus. I think that everyone there thought that they knew what was in his mind. In another family it would have seemed horrible, but in this one it was only natural.

"Nothing will happen to me," said Nero, "before it happens to you. Don't forget that, my sweet brother."

"I was only thinking of what might happen to anyone in a drunken brawl," said Drusus, "just by the way of cautioning you because of my brotherly love for you."

Nero ignored that one. "The old goat will have to make me his heir now."

"I don't see what else he can do," said Agrippina. "He hates us and he would like to destroy us as he did your father, but he does not dare, the legions and the people would tear him to pieces."

"How about Uncle Claudius?" asked Caligula.

"He's a half-witted fool," said Nero. "Tiberius would never inflict him on the Roman people."

"What makes you think he'll inflict you?" inquired Caligula. "At least, Claudius wouldn't rule from a *lupanar*."

Nero reached for another saltcellar.

"Children!" screamed Agrippina.

Chapter XII

A.U.C.776 [A.D. 23]

✠   ✠

THE MAIN streets of Rome on a pleasant morning were, at the time of which I write, much as they are today: busy thoroughfares filled with jostling crowds moving in both directions, opening for the passage of the litters and the sedan chairs of the rich and powerful and closing again behind them, as the waters of the sea divide before the prow of a ship and, after it has passed, reunite, leaving no sign of the wound other than the momentary scar of the wake.

So narrow and so crooked are the streets of Rome that no wagons or carriages are permitted upon them during the first ten hours of the day, a traffic regulation to which there are but few exceptions. But even so, early in the morning, the great throngs of pedestrians, the litters, and the sedan chairs often

cause congestion as they converge upon the Forum,
the heart of the great city.

It was so on a morning some two weeks after my
liberation from the Tullianum as I was returning
along the Vicus Tuscus after completing an errand
upon which Agrippina had sent me. I was wondering, as I often had, why the old girl so often chose
me to bear her messages or to execute small com-
missions for her, rather than one of her own numerous personal slaves. It wasn't because she loved me.
Perhaps it was because she had learned that I would
carry out her instructions with dispatch and intelligence; but more likely it was in the hope that
something would happen to me and that I should
never return.

The streets were filled with that heterogeneous
mass of humanity that wages its bitter, eternal
struggle for existence in poverty, in squalor, in vice,
in crime, in riches, or in luxury within the walls of
the capital of the world: unimportant little clerks
scurrying importantly hither and thither; tall,
blond Gauls; bearded Germans with their red-dyed
hair and rough tunics of the skins of the wild beasts
of their forests; togaed Greeks, moving with conscious dignity and, I am sure, a feeling of contempt
for their upstart conquerors; sleek, brown, shifty-
eyed Egyptians; bearded Jews; black Ethiopians;
ragged plebs; soldiers; sailors; hawkers; beggars.

As I approached the Basilica of Julius, I was
forced to stop while a great man passed in his litter

borne by four slaves. He was a magistrate, and preceding him were his lictors, carrying the fasces symbolic of his authority, while surrounding or following his litter were other slaves and freedmen attached to his family and the sycophants and parasites who were included in the considerable number of clients to whose support the great man must contribute.

No sooner had pedestrian traffic been permitted to move again after the passing of the magistrate and his retinue than it was again held up by the approach of another litter, the curtains of which were tightly drawn, doubtless to conceal from the view of the common herd the features of some noble Roman lady.

The litter was accompanied by a few slaves and freedmen who acted as a guard, pushing aside whoever chanced to obstruct the passage of the favored one. As it came opposite me, I saw the insignia of Helvidius Pius painted upon the litter, and immediately I was all eyes, for several female slaves walked beside it.

Suddenly my heart behaved in a most ridiculous fashion, seeming, apparently, to be essaying the impossible feat of mingling with my tonsils—for there was Attica!

I called her name aloud. She turned in surprise and looked at me, and when she recognized me, her little chin went up in the air and she marched past me with her eyes straight to the front. My heart dropped. I should not have been surprised had I heard it splash upon the pavement.

I was dumfounded. What had I done to deserve so cruel a cut as this? I racked my brain. I had done nothing—other than to have just barely missed crucifixion because of having saved her from two thugs.

So this was the sort of fickle baggage I had almost given my heart to! Almost? If not completely, why was I so depressed? I determined to put her from my mind and never think of her again, whereupon I proceeded to think of nothing else. Argue as I would that I was most fortunate to have found her out before it was too late, my obsession with the subject and my hideous mental depression might have suggested to a more acute intelligence that it already was too late.

I was in no pleasant mood when I reached home, nor did Caligula's greeting tend other than to increase my irascibility. "It's about time, slave!" he snapped. "One day you will keep Caesar waiting too long while you loaf and idle about the streets of the city. You will exhaust Caesar's patience, and then——"

"Caesar! Caesar! Caesar!" I mimicked. "Leave me alone!" I fairly shouted, "or Rome will be better off by one less Caesar."

It is seldom that I so lose self-control, but the edges of my temper were raw, and Caligula had applied an abrasive. With the passing years, he had become more and more irritating as his true character developed. What it might lead to, unless I kept myself well in hand, the gods alone might know. It was increasingly a question with me as to whether I should keep most in mind the crosses along the Via Flaminia or the fact that I was the great-grandson of Cingetorix. The two points of view were never in pleasing concord.

Of course, we were still both boys, and much of Caligula's bombast was but the empty boasting of a child. Our clashes were soon forgotten in a game of backgammon or dice, a visit to the Praetorian Camp or to the stables of the Green syndicate where the charioteers, trainers, and stable boys made as much of the nephew of the emperor as the soldiers did of the son of Germanicus.

Yet, subconsciously, these clashes must have had some effect upon our long-standing friendship: more upon the attachment of Caligula for me than upon the sentiments that I entertained for him, which, I must confess, are rather difficult to explain. When he had been a little fellow, I had felt a certain affection for him, and, as the years passed, something very much akin to loyalty, but these sentiments had always been clouded and oftentimes absolutely obscured by the contempt I felt for him.

Caligula, I am sure, never felt true, unselfish affection or loyalty for anyone during the entire course of his life. He realized that I was extremely useful to him, and that was about as near to affec-

tion for me as he ever came. Also, he was an arrant
coward, morally and physically, and all his life he
was afraid of me. It may sound ridiculous to say
that a Caesar was afraid of a slave, but I know that
it was true, and not even his mother knew Caligula
as well as I knew him. The very fact that I never
bent the knee to him, either literally or figuratively,
even after he became emperor, and that I said to
him with impunity what not even the most powerful
senator would have dared say, and that I outlived
him, proves my point.

It is true that he was constantly threatening me
with scourgings, exile, the mines, or crucifixion, but
it is also true that he never once carried out a single
threat to punish me.

And so it was upon this occasion that Caesar
subsided and that presently we were upon good
terms again, though I am afraid that I was not the
best of company that day. I could not keep my
thoughts from dwelling on the strange and inexplicable attitude of Attica upon our meeting in the
Forum. In a score of ways I sought to explain it:
someone had carried false tales of me to her; she
loved Numerius and this was her way of showing
me that she no longer desired to see me. But I knew
that all this reasoning was specious, for it was based
upon the ridiculous assumption that Attica had
entertained toward me a sentiment stronger than
friendship or that she knew that I loved her. She
couldn't have known any such thing, for I had just

learned it myself—to my sorrow. And as for her feeling anything more than friendship for me, that was quite ridiculous. She scarcely knew me. She might have felt gratitude, but one might feel gratitude toward a perfect stranger who helped one to his feet after having fallen in the mud. However, one would not of necessity have to fall in love with the stranger, nor even fold him to one's bosom as a friend.

On the other hand, love would not necessarily be engendered in the heart of the stranger. How came it, then, that I had fallen in love with Attica? It was all very confusing, especially when I analyzed Attica's cruel snub. It must have been a reaction to something, but a reaction is only as violent as the state which it attempts to oppose. Therefore, Attica's act presupposed a former sentiment toward me much stronger than friendship; but such an assumption was ridiculous. I gave the whole thing up as insoluble, and determined to give it no more thought.

I was still thinking about it a week later when a solution offered itself.

Following the death of his son, Drusus, Tiberius shut himself up in a remote part of his palace, refusing to see anyone. He was inconsolable, nor had he many friends to offer consolation with sincerity, so successful had been the fulminations of Agrippina and her party against him.

After the trial of Piso upon the ridiculous charge

of having poisoned Germanicus, near the end of
which Piso committed suicide, Agrippina and her
adherents were inflamed to fury because, through
the intervention of Livia, the Empress-Mother, the
accused's wife, Plancina, had found protection.

Night after night I had to listen to the brazen
conspiracies of Agrippina and her followers to un-
dermine the authority of the Emperor and place the
half-crazy wastrel, Nero Caesar, upon the imperial
throne. It is impossible that knowledge of this trea-
son could have been kept from Tiberius, and yet so
patient and forgiving was he that he took no step to
end these seditious activities for six long years.

During these years, Lucius Aelius Sejanus, whom
rumor linked with Livilla in the murder of her
husband, the son of the emperor, wormed his way
further into the confidence of Tiberius until he was
second in power only to the Emperor himself and
unquestionably was planning to succeed him. As
commander of the praetorian cohorts he was justly
feared by all, especially by Agrippina, who knew
that she and her sons were the greatest obstacles to
the fruition of Sejanus' grandiose ambition.

It was in this atmosphere of intrigue, fear, and
hatred that the imperial family lived, and the effect
upon their ill-balanced minds may easily be imagined. They saw poison in every cup, a dagger
beneath every tunic. The great hope that sustained
Agrippina was that one day she would be empress-
mother and reign as regent during the minority of

Nero Caesar and thereafter as the power behind the throne.

Every nature of foul gossip was spread by one faction against the other; perhaps the most preposterous were the whispered calumnies against Agrippina's morals. As you may have gathered, I had little love for Agrippina. She was haughty, arrogant, cruel, bitter, half-insane, and wholly dominated by a fanatical desire for power, but morally she was above reproach. Even the sainted Livia could lay claim to no greater purity.

I loathed the atmosphere that permeated the palace of Agrippina. It seemed that I breathed suspicion, hatred, and intrigue, and my state of mind was not improved during the week that I brooded over the cruel slight put upon me by a little slave girl. But what was I to do? I was a slave. If I ran away, death or the mines would be my portion were I caught, as I most assuredly should have been; yet, boylike, I used to lie awake nights dreaming of leading such an insurrection as that of the gladiators and slaves under Spartacus, which had terrorized all of southern Italy nearly a hundred years before. But when I reflected that after their defeat six thousand of them had been crucified along the road from Capua to Rome, I decided to cast about for something less spectacular.

If only I had had some hope of happiness in the future! If I could have but looked forward to an occasional hour of relaxation in the company of—well, somebody like Attica. Not Attica, of course: I had put her entirely from my mind. But where was I to find anybody like Attica? There was probably no one like her in the whole world, and certainly not in the household of Agrippina Major. Water clocks stopped when any of Agrippina's female slaves approached. There had been some rather cute ones before Nero and Drusus approached manhood, but after that, Agrippina got rid of them as fast as she could.

I was brooding over my sad lot one day in the garden behind the palace when one of the clock-stoppers approached. As she saw me, she stopped suddenly. "Well, of all things!" she exclaimed. "Here I've been carrying this letter around for I don't know how long, and never thought to give it to you." She reached inside her tunic and drew out a folded piece of papyrus. I took it from her. Who would be writing me a letter? Breaking the seal, I opened it. It was dated three weeks before, and started,

"To Britannicus,

"From Attica,

"Greetings:"

I could have, with pleasure, murdered that fright of a slave woman. I shall always think that she had deliberately withheld the letter from me, influenced by that turpitude which flowed from the head of the family to pervade the entire household to a greater or lesser degree.

"I have just learned, dear Britannicus, of your trial, condemnation, and pardon, and, for the last, may the blessings of the gods be upon Tiberius. You must have thought it strange that you had no word from me, the innocent but nonetheless actual cause of your persecution, but believe me, dear Britannicus, had I known, I should have come to you at once. I must see you, and soon, to express again my gratitude for all that you have suffered on my account. Between the sixth and seventh hours, my mistress takes her siesta. At that time I am free, and if you care to see me again after all the sorrow I have caused you, you will find me strolling on the Via Appia between the house of Helvidius Pius and the Capena Gate at that hour on the morrow and the day after. But if your duties are such that you cannot come, I pray that you will dispatch a letter to me suggesting some other plan."

Now I knew why Attica had snubbed me that day, nor could I blame her. From nadir, my spirits rose to zenith. I leaped to my feet and ran to the sundial, which confirmed my guess that the day had entered the sixth hour. Waiting for no permission from either Caligula or the majordomo, I bolted from the palace and ran all the way to the house of Helvidius Pius. I knew that Attica would no longer be strolling along the Via Appia waiting for me after three weeks, during which I had apparently flouted her sweet and generous advances; so I went directly to the side door of the house of Helvidius Pius and

pounded on it as though I were a messenger from
Tiberius himself.

Presently it was opened by a sour-faced Egyptian
slave, who eyed me scowlingly. "What do you want,
slave?" he demanded, "pounding thus upon the
door during the siesta hour."

"I want to see Attica," I replied.

"Get thee gone!" he growled, and tried to shut
the door in my face, but I stuck a foot in it so that
he couldn't.

"I must see Attica," I insisted. "It is important."

"And who are you to demand to see a slave of the
house of Helvidius Pius, and a female slave at that?
This is no lupanar."

"I am Britannicus, the slave of Caius Caesar
Caligula, and if you know what's good for you,
you'll take word to Attica at once."

"Well, why didn't you say so in the first place?"
demanded the fellow. There are castes even among
slaves, and the slave of a member of the imperial
family ranks high. "Wait here," he said. "I will go
and find Attica."

He came back presently with a sneer on his ugly
face. "Attica says that she never heard of you," he
said. "You'd better be running along."

I walked back to the Palatine Hill with my tail
between my legs.

Chapter XIII

A.U.C.776 [A.D. 23]

✠   ✠

I DEVOTED all the rest of my leisure time that day
to composing a letter to Attica. In fact, I composed
eight; the first seven I tore up. The one I finally
dispatched was far less flowery and hysterical than
its predecessors. It merely explained that the reason
I had not met her on the Via Appia was that her
letter had only been delivered to me this very day,
and that I had then immediately run all the way to
her house in the hope of seeing her. I asked her if
she would not send word that I might see her soon
and where. It was a much more dignified letter than
the others, probably such a letter as Cingetorix
might have written—had he been able to write. I
found a small boy on the street and gave him a
sestertius to deliver it.

I expected an answer in about an hour. I did not

get one. I did not get one the next day. I never got
one. I seriously contemplated opening my veins on
the doorstep of the house of Helvidius Pius. I
pictured Attica's remorse when she found me there.
It was very touching; then Caligula came and said
that we were going to visit the stables of the White
syndicate, and I decided to postpone my demise. I
was so fond of visiting the stables of the various
racing syndicates that I would forego any other
pleasure for the opportunity—even death.

"Why the White stables?" I asked. "I thought
you were devoted to the Green."

"I have just heard that they have some new
horses," he replied, "and I want to have a look at
them. They are going to work them out late this
afternoon, when it is cooler."

We found Tibur. Either he or some other praetorian had to accompany Caligula whenever he went
abroad; and when it was Tibur, we were both glad,
for we three fraternized like equals; many of the
others were fearful or obsequious: close association
with a Caesar affected them strangely. But not
Tibur. He was always the ex-gladiator whom multi-
tudes had worshiped. I have always thought that
having Tibur and me for his closest associates had a
beneficial effect upon Caligula for many years. Had
we been the usual run of fawning sycophants who
ordinarily surrounded Caesars, there is no telling to
what lengths he would have gone much sooner than

he otherwise did after he became emperor and was surrounded by boot-lickers.

Tibur and I both treated him as we would have treated any other person. When we thought he was wrong, we didn't hesitate to tell him so, and when he got up on his high horse, as he occasionally attempted to do, we dragged him down. I won't try to say that he liked it because he didn't, but he had to take it, and it developed a little more character in him than he would otherwise have had. I feel sure that if Caligula's mind had not been warped by heredity, Tibur and I would have made a good man and a great emperor of him; for, strange as it may sound, he really tried to deserve our approval.

As it was quite a little distance to the White stables, Caligula ordered out a litter, beside which Tibur and I walked until we were out of sight of the palace; then Caligula bade us both get in. It would never have done to have chanced letting Agrippina see a legionary and a slave crowding into a litter with a divine Julian. And it was crowded. Tibur was as big as a gorilla, and I was no midget even then. The four husky slaves knew that they were carrying something, but they seemed to take it all in good humor. Their black faces wreathed in smiles.

As we passed through the streets, many people recognized Caligula and called to him affectionately, and he smiled and waved to them. I saw many a broad grin as his companions were identified. This evidence of democracy in a boy Caesar endeared

him to those who witnessed it, nearly all of whom
would live to curse the day that he was born.

Tibur, too, was recognized, and many were the
good-natured, if coarse, jokes that were called to
him. He gave them back in kind and coarser. The
Roman populace is not overnice in its repartee.
Caligula enjoyed it all immensely, but soon we were
out of the crowded district and approaching the
stables of the White syndicate.

The plant of the White syndicate covered an area
of several jugeri; in addition to the stables for the
horses, the building that contained the chariots,
harness, and other equipment, and the barracks for
the stable boys, there was a track complete with
spina and goalposts where the teams were exercised
and trained. This track was the same width as that
of the Circus Maximus but much shorter, for, after
all, it is not in the straightaway that races are won
or lost, but in rounding the goalposts.

The superintendent of the White syndicate was a
freedman named Publius Scorpus, who as a young
man had been a famous charioteer, thus winning his
freedom. He was quite impressed by this visit by a
young Caesar, and went to great pains to impress
upon Caligula the excellence of the equipment and
the records of his horses and drivers, for a syndicate
which won the favor of a Caesar gained in populari-
ty with the masses.

"I understand," said Caligula, "that you have

four new horses belonging to Helvidius Pius, and I have come to see them work."

"I am only waiting for Numerius," explained Publius Scorpus, "who is training them and will race them in the next games held in the Circus. He should have been here before now."

"I would see the horses while we are waiting," said Caligula.

Publius Scorpus had them led out by stable boys, four beautiful chestnut stallions. I think I have never seen such gorgeous animals, nor a team so perfectly matched. Caligula went into ecstasies over them.

"They cost Helvidius a pretty fortune," said the superintendent. "His agents searched for two years before they were able to match up so perfect a team. The two from Mauritania were purchased two years ago as three-year-olds, the other two were found this year, one in Greece and the other in Spain; one is five years old, the other six."

"I would see them run," said Caligula.

"The moment that Numerius arrives," said the superintendent.

We waited. The sun was dropping lower and lower. Soon it would be too late. Caligula became more and more impatient.

"Let someone else drive them," he said. "I tire of waiting."

"There are no drivers here," explained Publius

Scorpus, "and I would not dare trust them to a stable boy."

"You mean to say that you have no one here who can drive a four-horse team?" demanded Caligula.

"I am the only man here who has driven a race," replied Scorpus, "but since my last race, many years ago, my left arm has been almost useless."

"I can drive them," I said.

Publius Scorpus looked at me with all the contempt that a freedman can bestow upon a slave. "You?" he exclaimed. "What makes you think you can drive a four-horse chariot? Is it because you have watched a few races?"

Caligula looked equally as skeptical as Scorpus, but Tibur grinned and nodded his head in approval, for he knew what Caligula had doubtless forgotten in his own egotism.

"What makes him think he can drive a four-horse chariot!" repeated Tibur. "He, the great-grandson of Cingetorix, who drove his father's war chariot in battle from the time he was eight years old—what makes him think he can drive a four-horse chariot? He drove them with razor-sharp blades extending from each hub, such chariots as only a master charioteer could maneuver with safety to the horses and men of his own people. And he did this with wild, half-trained horses. With these gentle old cart horses he could sleep halfway around the track."

"That is right," said Caligula. "I had forgotten. Let Britannicus drive the four."

"But——" objected Scorpus.

"No buts, man," snapped Caligula.

"If anything should happen, what would Helvidius Pius say? I should lose my job, and maybe worse."

"My uncle, the Emperor, would give you a better job. I wish to see the horses work. I wish to see Britannicus drive them—I, Caius Caesar Caligula!"

Scorpus delayed as long as he dared, evidently hoping that Numerius would come, but at last the horses were harnessed to the chariot, and I took my place, the reins knotted about my waist.

The stable boys at the horses' heads leaped aside and we were off. It was indeed a splendid team. The six-year-old, the horse from Greece, was on the inside. So sensitive was his mouth that with my little finger I could rein him. He was magnificent. I circled the spina seven times, and each time you could scarcely have thrust your hand between the hub of the chariot and the metae as we made the turn at each end. It was no test of driving, as there were no other chariots, and a child could have driven that perfectly trained team.

Scorpus breathed a sigh of relief as I drew rein in front of the little knot of onlookers. "You drive well," he said, as I dropped from the chariot and the stable boys led the horses away to be rubbed down and blanketed.

"You drive magnificently," said another voice in the rear of the other spectators.

I looked and recognized Numerius. I thought that the fellow must be pretty sure of Attica to praise a rival thus, but I acknowledged his compliment graciously. "The praise should go to the trainer of the horses," I said. "A fool could have done what I did."

"I think one did," said Numerius.

The fellow had insulted me! I could feel the blood recede from my face. I took a step toward him, and then Numerius smiled. "Wait!" he said. "Come to one side and let me explain; then you will probably agree with me."

We walked away out of earshot of the others. I was still angry, and Numerius was still smiling, as though he enjoyed my discomfiture.

"Why did you call me a fool?" I demanded.

"Because you are one," he said. "Why didn't you come to meet Attica when she wrote you? You love her. Any fool could see that when you were within sight of her. Then why didn't you come when she sent for you? That is why I called you a fool."

"But I thought you loved her," I said.

"I do," said Numerius, "but if I can't win her fairly, I do not want her at all. I do not want a wife who loves another man."

"But she loves you," I said.

"Not yet," said Numerius, "nor does she love

you—yet. Why did you not come to her when she wrote you?"

I explained the whole matter to Numerius. "I shall tell her," he said. "It is evident that the boy you paid to bring that last note to her took your money but did not deliver the note. Attica never received it."

"Why do you tell me these things?" I asked.

"I like a contest," he said. "At the games, I like to ride through the Gate of Triumph with the palm of victory in my hand. So, I would like to win in the game of love; but to win with honor, one must have a worthy rival."

"Then it is a contest?" I asked.

"It is," he said, "and may the better man win."

We shook hands on it, and from that day we were fast friends and eager rivals for the hand of Attica. There never was a finer man than Numerius, nor a greater charioteer.

Caligula called to me, and we prepared to leave. Scorpus shook my hand. "If Caesar will consent," he said, "you shall drive for the White."

"He is going to drive for the Green," said Caligula. "Green is my color."

Chapter XIV

A.U.C.779–780–781–[A.D. 26–27–28]

✠   ✠

AMONG THE pages of my diary that were cast into the sea by Caligula were those covering the next few years, so the picture I shall paint must lack detail, as ships seen from a distance. We see the ships, but we do not see the men upon them, nor what they are doing, and no more can we hear their voices to know of what they speak.

I saw Attica as often as I could, and she and Numerius and I were the best of friends, but I could not see that either he or I advanced his suit. Attica was sweet to both of us; she treated us with a sort of maternal solicitude, chiding us and laughing at us as though we were little boys if we spoke of love. Sometimes it was most aggravating.

Numerius had a great advantage over me in the practical argument which he might have offered. He and Attica were both the slaves of Helvidius Pius, and their marriage would in no way have inconvenienced the master whose permission they must obtain. With me, it was quite different. Even had Attica been willing to marry me, I cannot conceive that either Caligula or Agrippina would have given consent.

In the 779th year from the founding of the City, I was twenty; and I thought that if I were not married soon I should be so old that Attica would not want me for a husband. One is never quite so old again as at twenty.

During these years I had driven occasionally for the Green in the races at the Circus. Now and then I had won. I should have won oftener had not the superintendent of the Green stables always given me his poorest teams. For that I do not blame him. He had old, experienced charioteers who had proved their mettle, so why risk a team or a race? Another factor that often lessened my chances of winning was my disinclination to resort to the foul and unfair practices which were encouraged among the drivers by both the syndicates and the populace. Every dirty trick to which a charioteer might resort in order to win, even though they might result in the injury or death of horses and men, was countenanced and applauded. It was typically Roman.

By now, Sejanus had gained a position in the Empire second only to Tiberius in power, for the aging Emperor leaned upon him for advice and counsel. There had been a time when this man had courted the good graces of Nero Caesar, whom Tiberius had named as his successor; but, with increasing power, he ceased to fawn upon the oldest son of Agrippina, and I believe that it was at this time that he formulated the plan to remove all obstacles that stood in his path to the seizure of imperial power upon the death of Tiberius. How close he came to success during the ensuing five years!

But at the time these events did not interest me greatly. How could I guess that in paving the way to the throne for himself, he was laying down a red carpet of blood over which Caligula would ascend it. It is not for a slave to concern himself with affairs of state.

At this time the intrigues of Agrippina and Nero were almost common gossip in Rome. The insane mother and the vain and brainless son could not decently await the natural course of events that must soon remove from the latter's path to the throne the sole obstacle that intervened—an old and ailing man; they must plot and contrive to hasten the end.

I recall an evening when a number of the conspirators were gathered in the peristyle of Agrippina's palace. Among them was Titius Sabinus, and from the balcony above I distinctly heard him say that he had bribed a certain freedman attached to the person of the Emperor to assassinate him.

The monstrosity of the suggestion, bringing years of exciting intrigue and plotting so close to the actual perpetration of a hideous crime, seemed to awaken the dull mind of Nero to some appreciation of the foulness of the thing that Titius Sabinus was planning, and I will say for him that he demurred, but Agrippina overrode him. Already she could see herself the mother of an emperor and the virtual ruler of the world. What heads would fall when that day came! Red would be the streets of Rome and red the yellow Tiber. I imagined that I could see the she-wolf licking her chops.

I was shocked and horrified by what I had heard. For years, I had been cognizant of treasonable plotting and veiled and secret threats against the life of Tiberius, but, like Nero, I was not wholly prepared for the actual fruition of these.

What was I to do? More than once had Tiberius befriended me. He had on one occasion saved my life. But what could a slave do? Even could I reach his ear, it was quite possible that he would not believe me and that I should die for my temerity. I scarcely slept that night from thinking and planning, but when morning came my resolve had been made.

Romans, as you know, are early risers that they may take advantage of the cool morning hours to transact the business of the day. Tiberius was no exception.

I presented myself early that morning at the

gates of the palace. I was quite the first person
there, but when I announced to the guard that I
sought an interview with the Emperor, they laughed
at me and tried to drive me away.

"Listen, if you know what is good for you," I
said. "You have only to have word taken to the
Emperor that Britannicus Caligulae Servus brings
word to him on a matter of life and death."

When they learned that I was the slave of a
Caesar, and Little Boots at that, they bent more
attentive ears. Finally they summoned an officer,
but he too was skeptical.

"Please," I begged, "only ask the Emperor if he
will see me."

At last he assented. It was fully ten minutes
before he returned. "The Emperor will see you," he
said, but before I was admitted I was carefully
searched for dagger or poison.

Tiberius was still at his morning meal when I was
conducted into his presence. I approached and
stood before him. I did not kneel. I am the great-
grandson of Cingetorix. That, I never forget. Tiberius eyed me with a half-amused, half-quizzical expression.

"What trouble are you in now?" he asked. So he
remembered me! As little as I admire Caesars, I
was thrilled.

"I am in no trouble, Caesar," I replied. "I have a
message for you that no other must hear," and I
glanced at the slaves and freedmen about him.

Perhaps some of these were already planning his assassination! The thought gave me strength to insist upon telling my story to none other than Tiberius.

The Emperor frowned. I thought that he was going to refuse my request. "You have befriended me on several occasions," I reminded him. "Once you saved my life. I am here to make a return in kind."

He seemed to grasp the gravity of that which had brought me, a slave, upon so hazardous an errand, for it would indeed have been hazardous to have intruded upon Caesar on some trivial pretext. He signed for the others in the room to leave; then he turned again to me. "What is your message?" he asked.

I repeated to him, word for word, that which I had heard the previous evening from the balcony overlooking the peristyle of Agrippina's palace. "For this I shall die when Agrippina learns what I have done," I said. "I only ask of Caesar that he will demand that I be accorded a humane death— not crucifixion."

"Agrippina will never know," he said, "nor will you ever be crucified while Tiberius lives. Go now, and never repeat to another that which you have told me."

I hurried home, and, so fortunate was I, that I am sure no one knew that I had left the palace that morning.

Tiberius struck quickly. That very day Titius
Sabinus was arrested and confessions were wrung
from several of the Emperor's freedmen, doubtless
by torture. Trial, condemnation, and execution of
Sabinus followed immediately. The Senate and the
people were shocked by the revelations of the trial.
Perhaps they did not like Tiberius, but they knew
that to exchange him for the weak-minded Nero and
the vindictive Agrippina would make conditions
infinitely worse.

In thanking the Senate for its prompt action in
condemning Sabinus, Tiberius said, "I live a life of
fear and solicitude, being in constant apprehension
of the plots of my adversaries," and though he did
not name these adversaries, all Rome knew that he
meant Agrippina and Nero.

At last the wily Sejanus felt that the power of
Agrippina had received a mortal blow, and he came
out into the open with a public statement which he
would not previously have dared make: "The State
is torn into two factions precisely as though we were
in a condition of civil war, and one of these factions
calls itself the party of Agrippina. It is high time
that energetic action should be taken against certain
of the heads of this party, so as to abate some of the
mischief they are working." Lucius Aelius Sejanus
was preparing to strike!

It was in this year that Sejanus persuaded Tiberius to retire to the island of Capri, nor was this
difficult as the aging emperor was tired of the

plotting and intriguing of his enemies, of the immorality and corruption of Rome, and had long looked forward to the time that he might retire to the quiet and peace of his beloved island. From Capri he issued his imperial decrees during the last eleven years of his reign, and never again set foot within the gates of Rome.

The Emperor took with him a few Romans of high rank, but most of his companions in self-exile were literary and learned men, mostly Greeks, in whose cultured society Tiberius found his greatest happiness, a fact which amply refutes the hideous calumnies spread against him by the mad Agrippina and her party and which are still current even today. The very vileness of the accusations against his morality prove their falseness. For twenty-four years Tiberius had lived in the limelight of immoral, intriguing, scandal-loving Rome, twelve of those years as emperor, where his every act was watched by the jealous eyes of unscrupulous enemies; yet never in all that time was a breath of scandal attached to his name. How ridiculous it is to assume that by moving to Capri he should, in one short year and at the age of sixty-eight, have become a vile, degenerate monster!

Shortly after Tiberius sailed for Capri, there occurred that which augured ill for the future welfare of Rome, though little could any of those who witnessed it have guessed the bloody tragedies it portended. It was the luncheon hour in the palace of

Agrippina. Caligula, Agrippina Minor, Drusilla, and Julia were eating with their mother. Another slave and I were the only others in the dining room at that time. Suddenly, without warning, Caligula gasped, choked, and slipped from his chair to the floor. I had been standing directly behind him, and I succeeded in catching him in my arms and breaking the fall, so that his head did not strike the hard marble of the floor.

He stiffened convulsively, choking horribly, white froth upon his lips. Agrippina rushed to his side. "A doctor!" she called to the other slave. "Summon a doctor!"

The other three children were terrified and began to cry. Agrippina sent them from the room.

Caius Caesar Caligula had suffered his first epileptic stroke!

It was not of long duration. It was over before the doctor arrived, and I had carried his limp form to his room. When the doctor came, Agrippina dismissed him. "Caius Caesar slipped from his chair," she told the doctor, "and I thought that he had hurt himself; but it was nothing. He is all right now."

When the doctor had left, she summoned me and the other slave who had witnessed the attack. She glared at us from those eyes which could be so terrible. "You have seen the crosses upon the Via Flaminia," she said. "You know that sometimes the tongues of those who talk too much are cut out before they are crucified. Remember, then, that you saw nothing unusual at luncheon today."

Why she didn't have us killed at once, I shall never know; but what she said to us preserved the secret of Caligula's first attack of the falling sickness quite as effectively. I very much doubt that the story of that first attack ever is recorded in history or elsewhere, other than in these notes of mine which are written in a sort of Notae Tironianae which only I can decipher.

Caligula was morose, moody, and depressed for weeks after this seizure. I often detected Agrippina watching him fearfully, and I think that Caligula noticed this, too, for he became very short and irritable with her. The home had never been a pleasant one; now it was worse. I wished that I might get out of it. Agrippina Minor did two years later. She got married. This was in 781. The creature was thirteen when she was married to Cnaeus Domitius Ahenobarbus, "a man of singular ferocity of temper." Some of the stories that circulated about him in Rome suggest that, if not a madman, he certainly was not wholly sane. Two incidents which lend color to my conviction occurred some ten years after his marriage. During his attendance on Caius Caesar, he killed a freedman of his own for refusing to drink as much as he ordered him; and once upon the Appian road, he suddenly whipped his horses and purposely drove his chariot over a poor boy, crushing him to death.

I only mention the man at all because the fruit of his marriage with Agrippina Minor was another male in whose veins flowed the blood of the divine Julians—a taint which placed him in line for accession to the throne.* Of him, Ahenobarbus is supposed to have said: "Nothing but what is detestable and pernicious to the public can spring from me and Agrippina." He may not have said this, and probably did not; but if he did, he was a prophet of the first order who knew whereof he spoke.

---

*This child was later the mad tyrant, Nero.

Chapter XV

A.U.C.782–790 [A.D. 29–37]

✠   ✠

THE YEAR 782 was one of tragedy for the family
of Germanicus. Livia, the mother of Tiberius, died;
though by some she was believed to have been the
mortal enemy of Agrippina and her house, her fully
warranted suspicions of the aims of Sejanus had led
her to urge upon Tiberius the wisdom of leniency
toward Nero and his mother, for, after all, they
were of the imperial family, and the proud Livia
could not endure the thought of an upstart such as
Sejanus supplanting them.

But with the death of Livia, the last barrier to the
ambitions of the favorite was removed, and he
struck quickly. Playing upon the fears of the aging
emperor, he persuaded him to write to the Senate,
complaining of the actions of Agrippina and Nero.

The Senate was thrown into consternation. Nero

Caesar had been named by Tiberius as his successor. Those of the Senate who took action against
him and his mother could expect no mercy should
he ever come to the throne. They did nothing.

While they were deliberating, Agrippina and her
party organized a demonstration. A mob surrounded
the Curia in which the Senate sat, shouting that the
letter from Capri was a forgery uttered by Sejanus
to effect the destruction of the house of Germanicus. The crowd milled about, carrying statues and
busts of Agrippina and her children and screaming
threats and insults at the Senate; and the Senate
was cowed. I was one of that organized "popular
demonstration." I had been detailed to carry a
statue of the odious Agrippina Minor; but at the
first opportunity, when I thought no one was looking, I tossed it into an alleyway.

The next day, the conspiritors were gathered in
the palace of Agrippina, congratulating themselves
upon the success of their coup and making plans for
Agrippina and Nero to hasten to the Rhine and
place themselves at the head of the legions quartered there, that they might march on Rome and
wrest the throne from Tiberius; but Sejanus had
not been sleeping. In the midst of the gay and
hopeful conspiracy, a detachment of the Praetorian
Guard burst into the palace and placed Agrippina
and Nero under arrest.

Agrippina was stunned, and for a moment she
was speechless; then she turned to the others in the

room and said, "This cannot be. The soldiers who fought under Germanicus and the populace of Rome who loved him will not permit this final indignity to be heaped upon his widow and his son." She did not burst into the tirade of invective that might have been expected, and she moved with great dignity, surrounded by the guard, which treated her with all respect. Nero blustered a little and made silly threats of what he would do when he was emperor, but presently they were gone, and the other conspiritors were scurrying off—rats deserting the doomed ship. I never saw either Agrippina or Nero Caesar again.

The hush they left behind them remained upon the house. Drusilla and Julia wept. Caligula sat staring at Drusus, who looked frightened, as did his wife. They knew that Sejanus had struck. Would Drusus be next? The other Julia, Nero's wife, showed no emotion. Perhaps she was glad to be rid of a brainless, dissolute, unfaithful husband.

The trial of Agrippina and Nero was conducted with the utmost fairness in a court presided over by Lucius Piso, a magistrate of unquestioned probity. The evidence against them was so conclusive as to leave to the court no alternative but to condemn them.

Agrippina was imprisoned in an imperial villa at Herculaneum and Nero was sent to one of the Ponza isles. Caligula and his sisters, Drusilla and

Julia, went to live with their grandmother, Antonia, and, of course, I went with my master.

Before the sentence of banishment was made final, Tiberius went to Herculaneum to talk with Agrippina that he might convince himself of the reality of her guilt. The Emperor was a kindly man who had showered favors upon the family of Germanicus and even sought to excuse and forgive the wretched return of ingratitude that Agrippina had vouchsafed him.

Here was such an opportunity as only a mad-woman could have cast aside, but instead of attempting to make her peace with Tiberius, Agrippina flew into a fury, reproaching and reviling him. So violent did she become that it was necessary for a centurion to restrain her, from which arose the story, improbable in the extreme, that Tiberius had caused one of her eyes to be beaten out.

Now, Tiberius had no recourse but to confirm the sentence of the court, and Agrippina was removed to Ponza as a prisoner of the state.

Our life in the home of Antonia was very dull. Caligula was now seventeen and starting to follow in the dissolute footsteps of his divine brothers. He seemed to be wholly lacking in the commonest decencies of normal men, showing absolutely no interest in the fate of his brother or his mother. Of the former he remarked that "if Tiberius were not an old fool he would have had him destroyed immediately."

Drusus Caesar could not conceal his evident gratification at the removal of Nero from his path to the throne. He was now next in line of accession, and he had but to await the death of the ailing Tiberius to become emperor of Rome. He could not await the natural outcome of events but must needs carry on the conspiracy against the life of Tiberius. Perhaps he was spurred on by fear of the machinations of Sejanus, which had already laid low his mother and his brother and might be expected to reach out and gather him in next; and if he held this fear, it was well grounded, for Sejanus was not idle.

As the wily favorite had seduced the wife of that other Drusus, he was now engaged similarly with the wife of Drusus Caesar and not without success. The silly girl revealed to her paramour the details of her husband's conspiracy against the Emperor, and in the year 784 Drusus Caesar was confined in the subterranean prison beneath the palace of Tiberius on the Palatine. In the same year, Nero Caesar died on the prison isle to which he had been banished. The story circulated in Rome was that he starved himself to death to escape execution by the hand of a common jailer.

Caius Caesar Caligula, an epileptic degenerate, was now the accepted heir to the throne of the Caesars, and immediately the sycophants began to fawn upon him—but they kept one eye on Sejanus. And well they might. The man had now removed every obstacle but one from his bloody path to the throne. I very much doubted that anything could save Caligula, but Antonia did save him. She, in common with all Rome, knew the hideous story of the poisoning of Drusus, the son of Tiberius, by his wife, Livilla, and Sejanus, her seducer; and she now sent all the details of that vile business to the Emperor.

Sejanus was arrested and condemned to death. His body was cast down the Gemonian steps, hooks were driven into the still warm flesh and the corpse was dragged about the city to be reviled and insulted by the populace. For three days the mangled mass was left to the bestial mob before it was thrown into the Tiber. Livilla, his accomplice, starved herself to death by the direction of her mother.

Two years later, in 786, Caligula assumed the manly toga at the age of twenty-one, and, according to Roman custom, he then shaved for the first time. It was in this year that he suffered his second attack of the falling sickness. He was about to retire, and I was alone with him in his room at the time. I attended him until the seizure was over. He was very weak and depressed. After a while he spoke: "The divine blood of the Julii!" His voice shook with loathing and contempt. Never before nor ever since did I hear a Julian speak in other than tones of reverence of the tainted blood that flowed in their veins.

Presently he looked at me, and there was a light

in his eyes that might have made another tremble. "Nothing happened tonight," he said. "If you cannot remember that, perhaps you can remember the crosses beside the Via Flaminia."

"You do not have to threaten me, Caligula," I said. "I know where my loyalty lies."

He nodded. "I should not have doubted you, Britannicus," he said. "You have ever been loyal to me. I sometimes think that you are the only friend I have."

"Do not forget Tibur," I reminded him.

"Yes, good old Tibur," he said.

Neither of us ever mentioned the matter again.

Shortly after this, word came of the death of Agrippina. She had starved herself to death in her prison. I have never had any doubt but that by this time she was a hopeless maniac. Antonia and the girls wept for a while, but Caligula showed no sign of sorrow. I am sure that he felt none.

Following the death of Agrippina, Tiberius had Caligula brought to him at Capri, where the old emperor might have the young prince under his constant supervision; and here he married him to Junia Claudilla, daughter of M. Junius Silanus. The next year, 787, witnessed the death of the profligate and insane Drusus Caesar in his prison on the Palatine. It is said that he was starved to death by order of Tiberius, but that I do not believe. The Emperor was neither a cruel nor a vindictive man. Had he been, he would have tortured and destroyed the entire family of Agrippina years before, for he surely was given sufficient cause.

At Capri was a Jewish chief, one Herod Agrippa, a man twice the age of Caligula, into whose companionship the young prince was constantly thrown. I believe that many of Caligula's excesses after he became emperor were the result of the teachings of this man who schooled him in the diabolic machinery of Asiatic despotism.

In A.U.C. 790, in his seventy-eighth year, Tiberius, feeling that death would soon overtake him, traveled to Tusculum to visit Antonia, the grandmother of Caligula, doubtless for the purpose of advising her in what manner she should counsel her grandson when he succeeded to the throne.

During the return journey, he fell ill at Astura, not far from Antium, but he later recovered and proceeded to Circeii. It was evident to all of us who were in his entourage that the old emperor was failing rapidly, but he even attended festivities inaugurated in his honor at Cerceii, though he afterward suffered an abdominal attack.

At Misenum, he entertained at dinner in his usual gracious manner; while at table, Charicles, his physician, pretending to take his leave, felt the Emperor's pulse. Tiberius doubtless guessed what use Charicles would make of the information he had gained, and continued the entertainment as though to give the lie to the physician's fears—or hopes.

Tiberius was right: Charicles hastened to Macro

the Praefect to inform him that Tiberius was close to death, and the word spread through the whole court. All was excitement. Messengers were dispatched to the armies to announce the death of the Emperor, but the Emperor did not die—that night.

In the morning he sent for Caligula and his grandson, Tiberius Gemellus. Caligula was the first to arrive in the chamber where the grand old man lay dying. As always, I had accompanied my master, but I stood outside the doorway as Caligula approached the bedside, and I easily overheard the conversation that ensued.

"My son," said Tiberius, "although Gemellus is nearer to myself than you are, yet both of my own choice and in obedience to the gods, I commend the Empire of Rome into your hands. I earnestly charge you to love and protect Gemellus as though he were your own son."

Caligula, whose back was toward me, muttered something which I could not quite catch, and then Gemellus came. Tiberius, his voice growing steadily weaker, spoke to him for a few moments, then sank back upon his pillows. I thought that he had died, and so did the boys. Gemellus ran from the apartment to summon aid, but Caligula remained, hovering above Tiberius like an unclean vulture.

Presently Caligula turned away and left the room, and I followed him into the corridors where he was surrounded by courtiers, who hastened to him to congratulate him. There was no word of regret at the death of Tiberius upon the lips of Caligula nor upon those of any other there, though the corridors were filled with men upon whom he had heaped honors and favors.

Into the midst of all this unseemly gaiety burst Evodius, the most trusted of Tiberius's freedmen, to announce that the Emperor had recovered from his faint and desired food. It was with difficulty that I suppressed a smile as I saw the expressions on the faces of the courtiers change from ingratiating smiles to sheer terror. Even Caligula appeared frightened. If Tiberius recovered, he might be punished for this breach of decency.

Summoning Macro, he hastened to return to the bedside of the Emperor; and again I accompanied him and stood just outside the doorway. Poor Evodius, unfortunately for himself, entered with Caligula and Macro.

Tiberius was breathing weakly as the two men leaned above him while Evodius stood just behind them. I saw Macro whisper to Caligula, who tried to get the signet ring from the dying man's finger. Tiberius clenched his fist to prevent it, and Caligula threw a pillow over his face and reaching beneath held the old man's throat until he expired. These things I saw with my own eyes, but I hastened away from that doorway as quickly as I could, lest Caligula should know what I had seen. That I had acted with rare judgment was demonstrated almost immediately, as Caligula ordered that Evodius be crucified at once, after having his tongue cut out.

Thus died the man whom I believe to have been the greatest emperor ever to rule over Rome; thus came to the throne one of the worst.

Chapter XVI

A.U.C.790–791 [A.D. 37–38]

✠　✠

LIFE NOW became a very different thing for me from what it ever had been before. My master was master of the world. Subject to his slightest caprice, he held the life of every man, woman, and child throughout the Empire in the hollow of his hand. Sycophants, who would not have wiped their feet on me before the death of Tiberius, fawned upon me, for they knew that I had been the constant companion of Caesar since his infancy. They knew that he trusted me and they thought that I had far more influence with him than I actually did; no one could influence the mad mind of Caligula toward anything that was good or decent. I might have influenced him for ill, but I was never so inclined. Gifts were showered upon me, but I refused them all—not, I am free to admit, through any scruples or fine sentiments, but rather because I knew that I should be expected to give for value received and that eventually that would lead to my undoing.

In a moment of rare generosity, Caligula offered to set me free, but after thanking him, I told him that I would rather be the slave of Caesar than a freedman. He took this as a compliment, for which I was thankful. However, my real reason for declining freedom was entirely different. Free or slave, I should still be at the mercy of the slightest whim of a youth who was already displaying many signs of insanity that were apparent to one as close to him as was I. As a freedman, I might arouse the jealousy of those who had seen the freedmen of Tiberius elevated to posts of importance and thus have enemies awaiting the opportunity to bring about my undoing. As a slave, none would be jealous of me. With the death of Tiberius I had lost the one and only man to whom I could look for protection were my life threatened. Now I must depend solely upon my own wits.

Still animated by that strange excess of generosity, Caligula elevated Tibur to the rank of tribune of the Praetorian Guard and placed him in command of the troops stationed at the palace. He could not have made a better selection. Tibur had married the daughter of a Greek woman who kept an eating house in the city—the same woman in whose home he had once planned to hide me. She and her daughter were virtuous and respectable women, and after his marriage, Tibur gave up his loose friends and forswore those periodic drunken orgies from which he used to return looking as though he had been shot from a ballista into a rubbish pile.

During the first months of Caligula's reign, he lived up to the fondest hopes of the Senate and the people. He released political prisoners from prison and exile; he exhibited great deference to the wishes of the Senate; he sponsored public games with lavish prodigality, and gave liberal largess to the troops; then he suffered the worst epileptic attack he had ever endured.

I was with him at the time of the seizure, and I was with him when he regained consciousness. If a man's eyes are the windows of his soul, I pray that you may never look at the soul of a madman through such terrible eyes as were bent upon me then. Terrible as they were, there was a question in them, and I knew that my life hung upon the answer that seemed expected of me.

"Caesar fainted," I said. "He is all right now. I think that perhaps it was something he ate at dinner."

Caligula nodded. I had said the right thing.

"I believe that you should rest now and try to sleep," I said.

He turned over on his side, hiding his face from me. There was a half-smothered sound from his pillow. Was it a sob?

Caligula was confined to his bed for some time,

and the Senate and the people were plunged into despair. They did not know what I knew—that the emperor of Rome was a madman. I knew it, because between long spells of depression and moroseness he used to rave to me of the plans he would execute as soon as he was up and about again: he would condemn all senators to death; he would have himself deified and temples should be erected throughout the Empire where he might be worshiped. There was much more, but presently I came to believe that they were only the ravings of a maniac that would soon be forgotten. Not all of them were.

During his illness I was delegated to convey to him the sad news of the sudden and unexpected death of his wife, Junia Claudilla. I sought to temper the blow as adroitly as I might, but it was a waste of effort and sympathy.

"Excellent!" he exclaimed. "I had been hoping that she would die; it saves me the necessity of finding the means to remove her."

I was shocked, but his next remark shocked me even more. "I shall now marry Drusilla," he announced.

"But Drusilla is your sister," I said.

"She is more than that," he replied. "She is a goddess and I am a god. It is only right and fitting that such a holy union should be consummated and the divine blood of the Julii forevermore remain uncontaminated by admixture with the blood of mortals. Am I a lesser creature than the kings of

Egypt who ever married their sisters?" The
teachings of Herod Agrippa were bearing fruit.

While I was shocked, I was not wholly surprised,
as it had long been apparent to the members of the
household that he was infatuated with Drusilla,
with whom, as with his other sisters, he had had
sexual relations since boyhood. I recalled that years
before, Antonia had caught him in bed with one of
them. However, I imagine that the old lady was not
too greatly surprised, as incest seems to have been
one of the prerogatives of the Caesars.

During the four years that we had been at Capri,
I had not, of course, seen Attica. We had carried on
a most unsatisfactory and one-sided correspondence, but at least we had kept in touch with one
another. As a slave in the imperial household I
frequently found those willing to carry a letter to
Rome for me, but Attica was less fortunately situat-
ed. Caesonia had married a man of no importance
and was no longer living in the home of her father,
so that it was only upon rare occasions that Attica
could find a bearer for her letters. Quite often it was
Numerius who found the means to dispatch her
letters to me. Attica wrote me of his many triumphs
in the Circus, and I occasionally had a letter from
Numerius himself, often describing some unusually
thrilling race, but always one in which he had been
defeated. He never wrote of his triumphs. In one
letter he assured me that he had not attempted to
press his suit for Attica's hand during my absence

from Rome and would not until I returned. "Then," he wrote, "you will have to look to your laurels." It is needless to say that Numerius was not a Roman.

At the first opportunity after our return to Rome, I went to see Attica. During the four years that I had been absent from home she had not changed, unless it were to become more beautiful; nor had she changed at all in the lack of importance that she seemed to place upon the, to me, all-important subject of love.

"Of course I love you," she said, but the light in her eyes was that of a sprite rather than of a nymph.

"Then, if you love me," I said, trying to ignore the implication of her elfin expression, "there is no reason why we should not be married at once. As the slave of the emperor, I am sure that I can get permission."

"But I love Numerius," she said. "I love ever so many people, but I cannot marry them all."

She saw that I was hurt, and she laid a hand gently upon my arm. "Please try to understand, dear Britannicus," she said. "I do not want to make a mistake that would ruin three lives. I am not yet sure."

I knew then what she meant: it was definitely between Numerius and me—and Numerius was my very good friend. I do not subscribe to the belief that all is fair in love and war. I am not a Roman.

A.U.C. 791 is a year that I would forget, but its

horrors have burned themselves ineradicably upon my memory. From his illness, Caligula emerged a madman, and from being the idol of the people, he became a creature to be feared and loathed.

He became subject to insomnia, and when he did sleep, his rest was disturbed by frightful dreams. Then he would sit up in bed and call for me, terrified by fearful hallucinations. Often he slept but three or four hours during the night, spending the rest of the time wandering through the palace, pacing the porticoes, awaiting the dawn, and always I must be with him.

During these long, tedious hours he rambled on continually and often incoherently, revealing mad, preposterous plans for the future. Many of these he forgot, but many he carried into execution.

Shortly after his convalescence he took Drusilla away from her husband, Cassius Longinus, and married her to a depraved creature named Marcus Aemilius Lepidus, from whom he almost immediately took her for himself, announcing that he proposed to marry her, although she was still the legal wife of Lepidus.

Rome, rotten as it was, was shocked, and indignation ran high. His act imperiled not only his own person but those of the entire imperial family, yet nothing could dissuade him. I was with him when his grandmother, Antonia, remonstrated with him regarding this and some of his other mad caprices, but he answered her contemptuously: "Everything is lawful to me, and I may do as I will to anyone."

Perhaps to show his displeasure at Antonia's interference and to flaunt his independence of her, he had her steward, Alexander Lysimachus, thrown into prison, notwithstanding the fact that Lysimachus had been a faithful friend of Germanicus, his father.

It was shortly after this that Antonia died, and the rumor circulated through Rome that Caligula had caused her to be poisoned. I do not know as to that, but I was with him in his dining hall when from a window he watched with utter indifference the burning of her body on the funeral pyre, after a funeral from which he had ordered all marks of honor to be omitted. But what else might be expected from one who had exhibited no sign of sorrow upon the tragic death of his own mother?

Now, on cameos and medals, the heads of Caligula and Drusilla appeared together. Plans for the marriage, which was to have been a most elaborate affair of a religious nature, were maturing.

"It is only fitting that it should be thus," said Caligula, "since a god is to wed a goddess, even as the great Jupiter wed his sister, Juno; and who can deny the divinity of the Julian family?" I can assure you that no one did, at least not in his presence.

And then the unhappy Drusilla died—of shame, many believed. She was the sweetest of Agrippina's

children and still little more than a child. She was
but twenty when she died.

Caligula was inconsolable. The funeral that he
decreed for her was of elaborate extravagance. He
demanded that she be deified and worshiped. Temples and statues were to be erected to her and
sacrifices made.

Caligula did not attend the funeral but hurried
off to his country villa at Alba, where he amused
himself at dice and with singers and dancers; yet,
more than ever in his life he had mourned another, I
think that he mourned Drusilla. For some time he
traveled through the cities of Italy and Sicily and
let his hair and beard grow to evidence his grief.

Upon his return to Rome, Caligula adopted Tiberius Gemellus, the grandson of Tiberius, whom
the dead emperor had decreed should be associated
with Caligula in ruling the Empire; and on the
same day, his nineteenth birthday, Gemellus assumed the toga of manhood.

It was obvious to me why the young emperor had
adopted the youth, for thus he could deprive him of
the rights decreed by Tiberius, since, as the boy's
father, Caligula had all-embracing legal rights over
him, even to the matter of his life. Nor did I have
long to wait before events demonstrated that my
deduction was well-founded.

It seems incredible that there can be a human
being totally devoid of decency, of affection even
for those of his own blood, in whose whole being

there is no trace of the milk of human kindness; nor can there be. Such a creature is not human; it is a monster. Such was Caius Caesar Caligula, Emperor of Rome.

Tiberius Gemellus was a delicate boy who had suffered for some time from an infection of the lungs, which resulted in a cough that the physicians were unable to overcome and for the relief of which he took a concoction having a strong medicinal odor.

At dinner one night, Caligula detected the odor of this preparation on Gemellus' breath and immediately flew into a rage—doubtless simulated. "What!" he screamed at the unhappy boy. "You fear being poisoned at my table? You suspect me, and you take an antidote? You fool! What precautions could prevail against me, your father and your emperor?"

Gemellus tried to explain that it was only the odor of the medicine he took for his cough that Caligula detected, but the latter commanded silence and ordered him from the room. A momentary hush fell upon the company. I suppose that even the creatures with which Caligula surrounded himself had vestiges of mercy. They all knew that Tiberius Gemellus was a pleasant, harmless boy. Caligula looked quickly around at the faces of his guests, a questioning challenge in his eyes.

"You acted wisely, Caesar," said Macro, quickly. "He who would take an antidote for poison must be thinking of poison." The implication was quite obvious.

"I have long suspected him," chimed in another of the sycophants, and after that there was a chorus of revilement heaped upon the character of the defenseless boy. Caesar looked pleased.

Caligula had another of his sleepless nights. I was about dead for sleep myself when dawn broke; then the Emperor sent for Marcus Bibuli, a tribune of the Praetorian Guard, dismissing me after the man arrived. I did not hear the orders that Marcus Bibuli received from the Emperor, but afterward I learned of all that happened.

Marcus went directly to the apartment of Tiberius Gemellus, where the lad was still in bed. "You have offended Caesar," said the tribune, "and he commands you to atone for the insult."

"I offered Caesar no insult," said Gemellus, "but if he imagines that I did, I shall be glad to atone. What does he want me to do?"

Marcus proffered his sword to the boy. "He wishes you to take your own life."

For a moment Gemellus was stunned. It was difficult for him to believe that such a cruel command had been issued even by the crazy Caligula, but then, he knew that Caligula was crazy. He must have known that it would be useless to plead. Perhaps he was too proud.

"I do not know how," he said, and knelt before

the tribune, bending his neck to receive the blade: "Strike, Marcus!"

The tribune drew back, shaking his head. "None may do it but you," he said, "for no man may shed the sacred blood of the Caesars."

Gemellus arose and held out his hand for the sword. "Tell me how I may do it most quickly and with the least suffering," he said.

Marcus Bibuli showed him.

Thus died the grandson of the Emperor Tiberius, courageously, as befitted one of the blood of the great Claudian.

Chapter XVII

✠　　✠

WHILE WE had been yet in Capri, before the death
of Tiberius, Caligula had carried on an affair with
Ennia, the wife of Macro, the man who had befriended him and, I am quite certain, saved his life
by interceding in his behalf with Tiberius. The old
emperor, convinced of the insanity of Caligula,
feared for the life of his grandson, Gemellus, and for
the fate of Rome should Caligula come to the
throne. I once overheard him say to Macro, when
the latter was pleading Caligula's cause, "Caius is
destined to be the destruction of me and of you all.
I am cherishing a Hydra for the people of Rome
and a Phaeton for all the world."

Caligula used to joke with me about Ennia. He
thought that he was doing something very smart by
seducing an older woman, the wife of one of Tiberi-

us' most trusted officers. "She thinks that by becoming my mistress," he told me, "she will acquire great power, something that all women desire. To bind her to me more closely, I have promised the fool that I will make her my empress when I become emperor." And so, after the death of Drusilla, Ennia looked to the Emperor to make good his promise; but she was doomed to disappointment.

Caligula was invited to the wedding of Caius Piso and Livia Orestella, and when he saw the bride he became immediately infatuated with her. At the wedding feast he had her placed upon the couch beside him and there openly made love to her. Piso was helpless. I watched his face. It was absolutely white, but he had to force himself to smile and make witty conversation.

Before the meal was over, Caligula carried the bride from the room and shortly thereafter married her; but in a few days he tired of her and divorced her. Two years later he banished her.

At another dinner, shortly after his marriage to Livia Orestella, Caesonia and her husband were among the guests. Caesonia, far from beautiful and the mother of two girls, was a notable wanton; and perhaps it was this very wantonness which appealed to the lecherous Caesar. Caligula showed her marked attention during the dinner, even taking her from the room for half an hour during the meal. Among decent people, the interim would have been one of strained embarrassment, but not so with the

depraved intimates of the ruler of the world. Even
Caesonia's husband showed no sign of resentment or
embarrassment, but, on the contrary, seemed quite
proud that his wife had found favor in the eyes of
Caesar. I, a mere slave, went cold at the thought
that Attica was the chattel of such as these.

After Caligula and Caesonia returned to the table, the conversation turned to the subject of beautiful women, and someone, I have forgotten now
who, remarked that Lollia Paulina, wife of Memmius Regulus who was in command of the army in
Macedonia, was very like her grandmother, who, in
her day, had been a noted Roman beauty.

Caligula immediately took notice; his eyes
brightened, and he insisted on hearing more concerning the charms of Lollia Paulina. "It appears to
me," he said, "that such beauty should not be
buried in Macedonia," and then he turned to one of
his officers. "Command Memmius Regulus to send
his wife to Rome." The following day he divorced
Livia Orestella and devoted his attentions exclusively to Caesonia—or almost exclusively. Never,
since puberty, had he been able to do without
women, and after his association with Herod Agrippa he had given increasing attention to young boys.

Neither the cares of state nor his matrimonial
adventures had encroached upon Caligula's interest
in the races, and now that he was emperor, I often
drove for the Green syndicate. Nor was I any longer
given the poorest team, with the result that I won

many races and was fast becoming one of the most
popular charioteers in Rome.

Caligula owned many horses, but his favorite was
Incitatus, a gorgeous animal of which I was very
fond. Caligula, however, seemed to fairly worship
him. He had a house built for him; he would not
permit that it should be called a stable. In it was a
marble stall with an ivory manger. The trappings of
Incitatus were of purple, and the brow band of his
bridle was studded thick with precious jewels. A
retinue of slaves attended the horse, and its house
was richly furnished. In the name of Incitatus,
Caligula often invited company to dine with him in
this house. I may say that the horse was far more
worthy of adulation than the master. I loved the one
and looked with contempt upon the other.

Caligula hated the Senate and loved to deride and
embarrass it. Once, at a banquet at which there were
many senators, he announced that he was going to
appoint Incitatus a consul. There was an uncomfortable silence, as the senators did not know
whether he were in earnest or joking. I could have
told them that he was not joking, as he had told me
seriously many times that that was his intention.

"Incitatus is far handsomer, far more intelligent,
and vastly more loyal than any of the knights or
senators," he said. "So why should he not be a
consul?"

I do not know why he did not carry out his plan.
Perhaps he forgot about it. He forgot many of the

mad projects with which he toyed from time to time. But he did make Incitatus priest to his temple. By far the majority of his maniacal acts were unpremeditated—the result of sudden excesses of fury because of jealousy or, again, just the caprices of a mad and vicious brain.

I recall once, when we were in the theater, Ptolemy, son of King Juba, entered in his purple robe of royalty, and all the spectators rose to stare at him. Caligula was infuriated that such an ovation should be given to another than himself, and, although he had invited Ptolemy to Rome and was his cousin, he put him to death.

Although but in his twenties, Caesar was fast losing his hair, and he was extremely sensitive on the subject—so much so that on several occasions when he came close to a man with a heavy head of hair, he would have him dragged off to a barber and have his head shaved. Would that his mad caprices had all been as harmless! But they were not. One day, in the amphitheater, he espied a very tall man who was known about Rome as Colossus. By comparison, Caligula was a runt and that was enough to arouse the Emperor's jealousy and anger. He gave orders that the man be sent into the arena to fight with a gladiator. Colossus killed the gladiator. This further infuriated Caligula, who ordered that another be sent against him. Colossus killed this one, too, whereupon Caesar commanded that the poor fellow be clothed in rags, dragged up and down the streets "for the edification of the women," and then butchered. He was envious of even so mean a person as this poor Colossus.

Again, the people wildly applauded a gladiator who distinguished himself while fighting in a light chariot. Caligula was incensed that another should receive such applause, and, in his anger, leaped from his seat. In doing so, he accidentally tripped upon the fringe of his toga and fell headlong down the steps. Scrambling to his feet, convulsed with rage, he shouted to the crowd, "A people who are masters of the world pay greater honors to a gladiator than to princes admitted among the gods, or to my own majesty here present in their midst!" Then he hurried away.

Both the people and Caligula tired of the innumerable games which the Emperor lavished upon the populace during the first year of his reign, and after squandering millions of sestertii in this manner, he embarked upon the most stupendous and extravagant folly that the world had ever witnessed.

Across the Baian Gulf, from Bauli to Puteoli, is a distance of some two miles, and this he ordered spanned by a bridge of boats. It could serve no commercial or military purpose and accomplish nothing more than to satisfy the vanity of a diseased mind. He collected every vessel upon which he could lay his hands, until the seaborne commerce of Rome no longer existed. There were no ships to bear grain, and all of Italy was threatened with famine, but Caligula never swerved from his purpose.

The ships were anchored side by side, and across them he laid a wide platform of timbers. These he covered with earth upon which he built a military road of hewn stones laid in concrete, and when the road was completed, he rode across it in full armor, followed by troops with their standards, proclaiming that he had conquered an enemy—Neptune!

At intervals there were numerous stations and post-houses, and to supply these with fresh water he had an aqueduct built from the mainland. It is little wonder that, with this folly, the lavishness of the games with which he bored the populace, and his other mad extravagances, within two years he exhausted the more than two billion sestertii (more than $100,000,000) that Tiberius had accumulated in the public treasury during a reign of twenty-three years.

Having charged into Puteoli in a coat of mail encrusted with jewels, which had been worn by Alexander the Great, and followed by his "victorious" army, he returned across the bridge the following day in a triumphal car, followed by "captives" in chains. These tokens of his synthetic triumph were royal hostages from Parthia, who were being held prisoner in Rome.

At the center of the bridge, he mounted a tribunal and addressed his soldiers, praising them for the greatness of their victory and declaring that the exploits of Xerxes and Darius paled into insignificance when compared with this, his mightier enterprise.

The whole silly business sickened me, as it must have every intelligent man who witnessed it; but the soldiers applauded, for he distributed money among them after the conclusion of his harangue and invited them and all others to a great banquet that he was to give upon the bridge and the ships that night.

If the building of the bridge and the puerile antics enacted upon it connoted the insanity of their author, then the aftermath of the banquet proclaimed its homicidal tendency. By midnight, everyone, including the Emperor, was quite drunk, and it was then that he commanded the soldiers to throw all of the guests into the sea. When the poor creatures, floundering in the water, sought to clamber aboard the ships, Caligula had them beaten off with oars, so that many drowned.

Of all the inhabitants of the Empire, none was in a better position than I to rid the world of this monster, and it was often that I was tempted to do so. All that restrained me was the fact that the man trusted me. It would take much to overcome that single inhibition, but in the end Caligula succeeded.

After our return to Rome, Macro fell into disfavor—a position which his wife, Ennia, had occupied for some time, the foolish woman having persistently reminded Caligula of his promise to make her his

empress. Macro, too, acted without tact in calling
Caesar's attention too often to the latter's obliga-
tions to him. These things annoyed the insane boy:
he did not want to feel obligated to anyone, for was
he not only an emperor but a god!

The end came one night at dinner, where Macro,
as was his custom, sought to restrain Caligula from
acting the part of a silly fool. When he laughed too
loudly at the jokes of the mimes or danced to the
music of the flutists, cutting foolish capers, Macro
would caution him to show greater dignity, remind-
ing him that he was emporer of Rome; when he
fell asleep at table, Macro awakened him.

At last Caligula flew into a terrible rage. "I am a
boy no more," he shouted to his guests. "Look at
this man. He conducts himself as though still my
tutor. I, who was born a prince, nursed by emperors, cradled in a cabinet of state, must, forsooth,
bow before an audacious upstart, a novice affecting
the airs of a hierophant", then he turned his mad
eyes upon Macro. "Go," he said, "to him who
taught you to insult me; Tiberius will be glad to
welcome you—and your wife. I graciously permit
you to go in your own way."

Macro was white as a sheet as he arose and left
the dining hall. I never saw him alive again: he and
Ennia opened their veins that night, and the next
day Caligula had all their children put to death. He
wished none to remain as reminders of his indebted-

ness to Macro and the foul manner in which he had repaid that debt.

I mourned neither Macro nor Ennia. The former had become an arrogant and dangerous power because of his hold upon the praetorian legions, which he commanded. Why he made no appeal to them, I shall never understand. Ennia was a faithless wanton, although, I think, quite harmless—only annoying. Now they were gone. Others had preceeded them. Still others would follow them. M. Junius Silanus, the father-in-law of Caligula was the next.

Silanus was proconsul of Africa and commanded the legion that was stationed in the province. He had been a trusted officer of Tiberius and was loyal to the Caesars, but he made the mistake of sending advice to a madman. Caligula recalled him from his command because of this; then, putting to sea, he ordered Silanus to follow him.

Silanus was an old man, the sea was rough, and he was subject to violent sickness; so he put back to port to wait for the storm to abate. Caligula thereupon charged him with wilful disobedience and with plotting against him, and demanded that the senator, Julius Graecinus, impeach him. Rather than besmirch his own reputation by such a shameful and unwarranted act, Graecinus refused, and Caligula had him put to death in revenge. Then he sent a message to Silanus, directing him to "take his compliments to the spirits of the dead."

This could have but one meaning, and Silanus

ended his own life by cutting his throat with a razor. Caligula had now removed all those close to him who might either reproach or advise him, with the exception of his two remaining sisters. It was soon to be their turn.

Chapter XVIII

✠ ✠

THE INFATUATION of Caligula for Caesonia gave me many opportunities to see Attica, as I was often sent to the home of Caesonia with notes or presents. Caesonia, knowing the close relationship that had existed between Caligula and me during practically the entire life of the Caesar, assumed that I had far greater influence with him than was the case. Consequently, she treated me with great kindness and indulgence, going out of her way to see that Attica and I had leisure to be together whenever I came to her house, and upon several occasions, when Caligula complained that I had absented myself from his imperial presence for too long a time, she took the blame upon herself, saying that she had detained me.

Caesonia was not alone in the belief that I was

something of a power behind the throne. Perhaps I
might have been, had I made the attempt, but I did
not. I knew Caligula better than any other, and so I
knew how advice irked, annoyed, and often infuriated him. I had seen what had happened to some of
his most loyal advisers, and I made it a point never
to offer it. Good advice, he would not have followed,
and he needed no one to advise him in matters of
ruthlessness and vice—of these he was a master.

Caesonia's house was near the Capena Gate, not
far from that of her father, and so the Via Appia
was still the favorite haunt of Attica and myself
when time permitted us the luxury of a long walk
together. Sometimes Numerius went with us; it was
a strange courtship. We often laughed together over
it. Numerius and I laid wagers on which one would
be successful. I put my money on Numerius and
Numerius put his on me. Attica laughed at us and
called us two silly little boys. We appointed her
judge and stakeholder.

"What shall I do with the money when I marry
another?" she asked.

We told her that she could keep it, as neither of
us would ever thereafter have need of money. "We
shall open our veins," I told her. That was a great
joke, and we all laughed.

Numerius was a Spaniard from Lusitania—very
dark and very handsome. He was extremely good-
natured and slow to anger—an attribute that I had
never considered a characteristic of Spaniards.

These things, with his good looks, his ready wit, and his fame as a charioteer, constituted him a most dangerous rival in an affair of the heart. Personally, I could not see how Attica could resist him—he had so much more to offer than I. Strangely enough, Numerius felt the same way about me: he told me so once when we were discussing our strange rivalry.

"It is too bad, Attica," I once told her, "that you were not twins."

"That would have been sad indeed," she replied, "for twins, being exactly alike in everything, would have loved the same man."

"Numerius couldn't have married you both," I said.

She just wrinkled her nose at me. I never could get from her even a faint suggestion of her preference.

"You are a little flirt," I said.

"Of course I am. No matter how much you men inveigh against them and deplore them, it is the flirts you run after—even Caesar."

"Especially Caesar," I corrected her. "But now you have made my little joke indecent. To mention you in the same breath with Caesar and Caesonia is sacrilegious."

She put a finger to her lips. "Be careful," she warned, "there is still room for more crosses on the Via Flaminia."

We were walking along the Via Appia beyond the

Capena Gate. I glanced quickly around to see if I might have been overheard. We were alone except for a fat milch cow tethered among the grasses that grew beside the road.

"There is no one else here," I said.

Attica pointed at the cow. "Do not forget the fall of Troy," she whispered dramatically.

"That was a horse, not a cow," I reminded her.

"Well, Greeks could hide in a cow as well as in a horse," she said.

"I wouldn't mind, if they were Greeks," I replied; "but a cow full of Italians would be something else."

"That would kill the cow," said Attica.

"Then we are safe," I said, "for that cow is very much alive. Now I can say whatever I wish; I can even shout it."

"I wouldn't," she warned me. "But what is it you want to shout?"

"I love you," I said. "I should like to stand on the roof of the Basilica of Julius and shout it to the world."

"You would look very silly."

"Have you no romance?" I demanded.

"I hope not, if it would make me as idiotic as you and Numerius sometimes are."

"Don't you want us to love you?"

There came then an expression in her eyes that I had never seen there before—sultry, desirous. It passed quickly, and now she was serious. "I think I should die if neither of you loved me," she said. This was a new Attica who left me speechless. I realized then that we had all been taking love too lightly, usually joking about it. Deep in my heart I had always felt that it was a serious, sacred thing, and in that fleeting instant I had looked into Attica's heart and seen my own conviction mirrored there. Attica and I never joked about love after that.

I did not know until long afterward that that walk beyond the Capena Gate marked a turning point in my life. Like other walks with Attica, it had been very delightful and was over all too soon. I saw nothing unique in it, but then men are proverbially blind.

When I returned to the palace that day, I found Caligula in one of his tantrums. First, he berated me for being away for such a long time. "I can depend on no one," he shouted. "Even my slave, who has been the recipient of my favors all his life, deserts me at a time when those closest to me are plotting against me. I shall have you and all the others destroyed. Have you forgotten that there is a Via Flaminia, Britannicus?"

"You have never permitted me to forget it," I said, "but only a fool would crucify the only man who has been loyal to him all of his life. Why are you surprised that someone is plotting against you? Has there ever been a Roman emperor, or, for that matter, any highly placed Roman, against whom no

one was plotting? Who is it now whom your spies
have turned up?"

Then he began inveighing against one of his
favorites, Lepidus. This Lepidus had been the husband of his sister, Drusilla. The fact that Caligula
had taken her away from him and lived with her as
her husband without dissolving the marriage had
not seemed to lessen the loyalty and friendship of
Lepidus for the man who had wronged him. I had
always looked with contempt upon Lepidus, consid-
ering him among the lowest of the fawning sycophants surrounding the Caesar; I was to learn that
he was but nursing his hatred and biding his time
against the moment of his revenge and the attainment of his amazing ambition, which was nothing
less than to become emperor of Rome. He was a
noble of the ancient and illustrious Aemilian family,
descended from an Aemilian who had been triumvir
with Augustus and Antony, though upon that alone
he could base no claim to the throne.

During his illness, in the first year of his reign,
Caligula had bequeathed his inheritance and the
succession to the throne to Drusilla; as she was still
the legal wife of Lepidus, he had had visions of
becoming emperor upon the death of Caligula. But
the Emperor recovered and Drusilla died. In his
disappointment, Lepidus planned to arrange the
assassination of Caligula, who, following his illness,
had brought upon himself the hatred of the Senate

and the people, the former by his insults, the latter by the burden of the outrageous taxes he imposed.

"The ramifications of the plot are widespread," complained Caligula. "They extend from my sisters here in Rome to Gaetulicus in Germany."

"You mean that Agrippina Minor and Julia are involved?"

"Lepidus has won them over. He hopes to marry Agrippina as soon as she can rid herself of Ahenobarbus, and then, when I have been done away with, he plans to claim the Empire."

"You are sure of all this?" I asked.

"I shall make myself sure," replied Caesar. "I am going to Germany. Gaetulicus is already there, and I shall take my sisters and Lepidus with me. Thus, I believe, I shall find the means of sifting this affair to the very dregs."

While discussing this affair he appeared quite rational. He flew into no fits of maniacal rage but laid his plans with infinite cunning after mature deliberation. I think that he realized that Agrippina, Julia, and Gaetulicus were too popular to be accused lightly or condemned without ample proof of guilt, and he now well knew that he was hated not only by the Senate but by the people.

Gaetulicus was that Cornelius Lentulus Gaetulicus who had long commanded the legions in Germany with such consideration for his soldiers that their first loyalty would be to him rather than to his brother-in-law, Apronius, who commanded the

legions on the Lower Rhine, upon whose support
the conspirators could depend.

If the suspicions of Caligula were well-founded,
the plot against his life and his throne had reached a
point of extreme seriousness requiring immediate
and drastic action.

During the journey to Germany, the Emperor, by
bribery and torture, wrung the truth from the slaves
and freedmen of Lepidus, Agrippina, and Julia. He
obtained much of the correspondence of the conspirators, and this correspondence, which I saw, fixed
the guilt of the principals incontrovertibly.

Arrived at the camp of Gaetulicus, Caligula
struck. Lepidus and Gaetulicus were arrested. The
conspirators were thrown into confusion. Agrippina
and Julia, knowing their own guilt, were terrified,
but Caligula took no action against them immediately. He left them in suspense, wondering how
much he knew and knowing that he was a madman.

The legionaries were restless and grumbling. Because of them and their loyalty to Gaetulicus,
Caligula's life hung in the balance. He was constantly guarded by the two cohorts of the Praetorian Guard that had accompanied him from Rome,
and Tibur and I were never permitted to leave him.

An arrant coward, he was terrified, but he acted
with the caution and wisdom of a sane man. Gaetulicus and Lepidus were brought to trial before a
military court over which the Emperor presided,
and thus the evidence that they had conspired to

take the life of Caligula was revealed to the army. They were condemned to death and almost immediately executed. The fickle soldiery, encouraged by a generous donation of money from Caligula, applauded the Emperor and heaped execrations upon the memory of Gaetulicus. The crisis was passed and Caesar breathed once more.

Shortly after this, he caused his sisters to be brought to trial upon charges of adultery and banished to the Ponza isles. With this solution of his problem he was quite pleased.

"I cannot charge my own sisters with plotting to have me assassinated," he told me. "If the world knew that Julians would cause the murder of a Julian, the example might influence others to attempt the same thing."

Caligula did not send his sisters into exile immediately, but kept them under arrest during his stay in Germany. He took from them all their hereditary honors and confiscated all of their personal property, including their slaves.

Having already spent the more than two billion sestertii accumulated in the public treasury by Tiberius, the Emperor was hard-pressed for funds and resorted to every artifice to raise money. Even before leaving Rome for Germany he had imposed a daily tax upon all prostitutes equal to their charge for one service. He even opened brothels in the palace and sent his agents to the Forum and the baths to solicit men, both young and old, by name,

to patronize these imperial lupanars as a mark of
loyalty to their emperor.

He sent for the slaves and household goods of his
sisters and auctioned them off to the rich provincials
of Germany and Gaul, himself describing the rarity
or the historic significance of many of the articles,
some of which had belonged to Antony, Augustus, or
his own father or mother. His cupidity and meanness knew no bounds.

Delighted with the success of these auctions, he
sent to Rome for all the furnishings of the palace of
Tiberius and auctioned these or whatever else he
could lay hands upon in the same manner. There
were many shameful incidents connected with these
auctions, many tragic and occasionally one that was
amusing. I recall one day when old Aponius Saturn-
inus fell asleep, and as he dozed his head would nod
forward and then snap back, only to nod again
almost immediately. Caligula noticed this and
called the attention of the auctioneer to it, remind-
ing him that each nod meant the acceptance of a
raise in the bid for the articles under the hammer.
When Apponius awoke it was to discover, to his
dismay, that he had bid in thirteen gladiators for
nine million sestertii.

But not even by all these expedients could Caligula raise sufficient revenue to cover his mad extravagances; so he must needs find other means by
which to replenish the depleted treasury. Nor was
that beyond the resources of his diseased mind

which, coupled with his unlimited power, made all things possible to Caesar. On trumped-up charges, he condemned wealthy men to death and confiscated their property. In one such case, his victim proving to have far less wealth than Caligula had supposed, he said to me: "I was deceived about him; he might have lived."

He caused a law to be enacted which required that he have a share of all fortunes left by will, and if a rich man kept him waiting too long for his legacy, he sent him poison. Under the rule of this divine Julian, I was glad to be a poor slave.

While we were in Germany, Caligula decided to win military glory by an incursion of the territory of one of the unconquered tribes beyond the Rhine. He coveted a legitimate triumph—he, the most arrant of cowards. He made great preparations and even crossed the river himself, but when a messenger arrived from the advance guard bringing a false report of the approach of the enemy, Caligula leaped from his chariot and, throwing himself upon a horse, raced back to the bridge. Finding this filled with the carts and sumpter beasts of the transport, he had himself passed from hand to hand above the baggage train until he reached the safety of the left bank.

I was so disgusted by this act of cowardice, as was the entire army, that I so far failed to restrain my tongue that it is a wonder that I did not ornament the Via Flaminia for what I said to

Caligula when he was safe within his tent. He was still wild-eyed and panting from his exertion as he asked, "Do you think the enemy will cross the river?"

"If he does not, it will be through no valor of yours," I replied, and then I added, "It was not thus that Julius Caesar fought."

"I was ill," said Caligula. "See that the word is spread that it was illness that caused Caesar to seek his tent." He was almost pleading. Suddenly he brightened. "I will show them," he exclaimed. "Wait! They shall yet see that Caius Caesar Caligula is a great general."

I did not know how he was going to prove it, but a couple of days later I witnessed the execution of his plan. It was at a banquet. Word was brought to him that the Germans had appeared, whereupon he leaped from the table and went out against the enemy at the head of his troops, a picture of stern, uncompromising valor. After some little time he returned with prisoners—members of his German auxiliaries whom he had caused to hide in a wood and be "captured."

Such exhibitions as these, together with the machinations of his enemies and the hatred of all classes of the people, had tended to alienate the loyalty and affection of the army. Both Tibur and I warned him of his danger, and he sought to win back the troops by lavishing upon them extravagant donations from the money derived from his auctions, his thefts, and his murders. But even this failed to quiet their unrest, and so he determined to compel their fidelity through terror. "I shall provide them such an example of my ruthlessness and power," he said, "that they will never dare rise against me."

"Be careful," warned Tibur. "Too many men hate you already."

"Let men hate me," exclaimed Caligula, "if only they fear me."

Tibur and I wondered what new turn his madness would take, and we were quite relieved when he summoned the most mutinous legion to gather to enjoy an entertainment and receive further largess. We thought that he had decided to propitiate the legionaries rather than to further antagonize them. He issued orders to their officers that the men should come without arms, and as they started to congregate they saw that they were being slowly surrounded by a cordon of mounted auxiliaries—cavalry recruited in the far provinces of the Empire—and then the truth leaked out: that it was Caligula's intention to have the entire legion massacred.

The soldiers ran to their tents and procured their arms, while Caesar fled. He did not slow down until he reached Italy, and he did not stop short of Rome.

He took his sisters with him. Ahenobarbus, Agrippina's husband, had died, and Caligula compelled

Agrippina to carry in her arms all the way to Rome the ashes of Lepidus, her lover. Such was the petty and contemptible meanness of the ruler of the world.

Chapter XIX

A.U.C.792 [A.D. 39]

✠   ✠

DURING THE return journey to Rome, Caligula was morose and irritable. He must have felt humiliation for his cowardly actions on the Rhine, and his thoughts played constantly with ideas of revenge. Afraid of the army, afraid of the people, he determined to launch the full force of his fury upon the unhappy Senate; and when an embassy of that august body met him upon the way to welcome him to Rome, he struck the pommel of his sword with his hand and exclaimed, "Yes, yes! I shall soon arrive in Rome and this shall come with me." Then he sent a proclamation which was to be posted on the walls of the city announcing that he was returning to his faithful knights and people, but not to the Senate that loved him not.

Shortly before we left for Germany, Lollia

Paulina, the wife of Memmius Regulus, had arrived in Rome from Macedonia, sent by her husband on orders from Caligula. The Emperor was greatly taken with her beauty, and after divorcing her from her husband, immediately married her. In a few days he discarded her.

Upon his return to Rome, he picked up anew the threads of his affair with Caesonia, and very shortly afterward he married her, an event which pleased me if it pleased no one else, as it brought Attica to live at the palace on the Palatine.

Caligula was still cursed with insomnia, and he used to pace the porticoes of the palace at night for hour upon hour. I never have suffered from insomnia, and I often had great difficulty in keeping awake as I drove my weary legs beside him. During these dismal, nocturnal vigils, Caligula customarily kept up a running fire of talk. It was seldom conversation, as I was rarely included in it. Often it was but muttering and grumbling. Occasionally he would laugh aloud, and his laugh was maniacal, horrible. I did not enjoy these midnight rambles, although I learned much from them that I might have used to my advantage had I been a politician.

Often he pretended that he was conversing with Jupiter, and, after speaking at length, he would cock his head on one side and listen to the god's reply, pursing his lips and nodding his head in simulation of complete understanding. At such times he would often get into violent arguments with

Jupiter, ending up by threatening the god with annihilation.

Again, he might take me into his confidence relative to the most intimate affairs, such as his relations with women, often expounding the physical attractions of his wife.

"I do not know why I so love Caesonia," he once said to me. "She is far from beautiful, she is the mother of three children by another man, and she is, furthermore, a notorious wanton. Perhaps it is that last characteristic which makes me love her, or perhaps she is giving me a love philter. I have often contemplated putting her on the rack to force a confession from her."

I once heard him say at a banquet, laughingly, as he touched Caesonia's neck, "When I give the word, this beautiful throat will be hacked through." Had he lived a little longer, I have no doubt but that Milonia Caesonia would have lived only a little longer than she did.

Caesar's humor was as baroque as his excesses and cruelties were extravagant, and he loved to embarrass senators, and even the two consuls, in public. He had less conception of the duties of a host than the meanest shepherd upon the outer slopes of the Janiculan Hill, and I believe that he invited great men to his table for the sole purpose of insulting them. Upon one occasion, when he had the two consuls as guests at a banquet, he suddenly burst into raucous laughter, and when one of them asked to be told the joke at which the great Caesar laughed, he said, "Oh, nothing but that at a single nod of mine you would both have your throats cut." The laughter of the consuls was pale and anemic.

His cruelties were such as could have been conceived only by a maniacal monster. He had senators and Roman knights whipped and tortured in his presence, not that he expected to obtain information from them, but simply because it amused him to see them suffer. Upon one occasion he had a number of such noble Romans beheaded by torchlight while he walked in his garden where he might watch the butchery. Death by whip and fire, the death of the common slave, was the lot of many a knight and senator.

He once told me, during one of those pre-dawn pacings of the porticoes, that he was planning to massacre the whole Senate; then he added: "I wish that the Roman people had but one neck, that I might cut it through with a single blow, thus relieving me of the necessity of doing it piecemeal and at different places." He often had an executioner in attendance at his banquets and had people beheaded for his amusement during the meal. How right was Tiberius in feeling that he was committing a great wrong in permitting Caligula to live!

But all was not blood and butchery. Caligula still enjoyed the chariot races in the Circus, though I often thought that he was disappointed if there were no fatal accidents. He would lean far forward, his eyes gleaming with suppressed excitement, as he watched a driver being dragged to death by four terrified horses.

I drove for the Green quite often now and had become a popular charioteer, as I won far more often than I lost. The cheers of my supporters followed me around the arena as I passed in review with the other drivers in the procession which always preceeded the races, and a storm of applause followed me as I drove through the Gate of Triumph with the palm of victory in my hand when I had won. But the adulation and plaudits of the Roman populace left me cold because of the contempt in which I held all Romans. A nod of approval from a barbarian Briton chief would have meant infinitely more to me than the acclaim of all the Caesars and their degraded subjects. I hope, my son, that when you are old enough to read these memoirs of mine that you will grasp the fact that I hold neither respect nor admiration for the Romans, a race of people whose only contribution to human "progress" has been the invention of new means for destroying human life and whose only noble achievements have been copied from older and nobler civilizations which they sought to destroy. Let it always be your chiefest pride that no drop of Roman blood flows in your veins.

Those days, as I have said, were not all horror. Attica and I were often together, which gave me the opportunity to continually urge her to reach a decision between Numerius and myself before we were all laid low by senility.

Once she said to me, "You race tomorrow against Numerius. Perhaps I shall reach my decision after that race." Had another than Attica made such a statement, I should have assumed that the winner of the race would be the winner of her hand, but I knew that Attica meant nothing of the sort. She was too fine to place herself as the amount of a wager, like so many sestertii. It was just her way of putting me off again. I supposed that my importunities bored her, so that she would adopt any artifice to win even a brief respite from them.

However, I could not but recall her words as the barriers were dropped the following day and the sixteen horses and the four chariots lunged onto the arena. It was the last race of the day, a race that I was confident I should win as I was driving by far the best team.

I had drawn the outside position, Numerius the inside, which gave him considerable advantage. As we were turning the far end of the spina for the fourth time, Numerius and the Red driver were racing neck and neck. I had maneuvered from the outside to the inside, where I was trailing directly behind Numerius; the Blue chariot was on my right, the noses of its horses opposite the rear of my car.

Numerius had not been urging his team, but I knew that he soon would and would draw ahead of the Red. I would follow through the opening, and when Numerius and I had left the other two cars in the rear and had the race to ourselves, I could pull to the right and easily take the lead and win the race in the remaining two and a half laps. My confidence was not based upon egotism: I knew my team and I knew that which Numerius was driving in this race. Mine so far outclassed his that there was no comparison.

Numerius was making a beautiful turn: one could scarcely have inserted a hand between his left hubcap and the second goalpost. The Red and the Blue drivers were urging their teams on with whip and voice; the audience was screaming encouragement, advice, and abuse at one or the other of us. I could imagine that Caligula was screaming with the rest, for I knew that he had wagered five hundred thousand sestertii upon me. It behooved me to win this race!

Then it happened! So much can happen in one or two seconds that it takes so long to tell! The Red driver crowded Numerius, turning in on him in an effort to pinch him off and take the lead. The two chariots crashed together, forcing the left wheel of Numerius' against the third goalpost. The Red swung away, his car undamaged, but that of Numerius rolled completely over on top of him.

I went absolutely cold. I could see no hope for him. In front of my eyes he would be dragged to death.

His horses, freed from all restraint, leaped ahead.
Then I saw Numerius lying in the sand directly in
my path. He had cut the reins even as his car rolled
over. To drive over him and win the race would
have been entirely proper and ethical by the standards of Roman sportsmanship. It would have given
the populace a great thrill and me, doubtless, a
tremendous ovation. It would also have given Caligula five hundred thousand sestertii. To throw the
race now might cost me my life; daily, Caesar was
destroying knights and senators on much less provo-
cation.

These things passed through my mind as I pulled
my team sharply to the right across the path of the
Blue. There was a crash, as horses and chariots
came together, and as my car rolled over I cut
myself loose. The Blue driver was not so fortunate.
I tried to reach him before those of his horses that
were thrown had lunged to their feet, but I was too
late and had to watch the poor devil being dragged
to death as his frantic team tore around the arena,
which was now full of stable boys attempting to
catch the three runaway teams.

I hurried to Numerius, who still lay where he had
fallen. He was only stunned, and as I dragged him
to the spina where he would be out of the way of
the flying hooves and reeling chariots as the Red
driver and the loose teams came around again, he
regained consciousness.

It was all a great show for the sadistic audience,

which was standing and screaming its approval. I wondered what was passing in the tortuous convolutions of Caligula's mad brain. I shuddered as I envisioned a cross beside the Via Flaminia. Even a Caesar does not lose five hundred thousand sestertii with any degree of equanimity.

As Numerius and I left the Circus by the little gate used by attendants and employees, I found Tibur awaiting me. His expression was most serious. "What's the matter?" I asked. "Who's dead? You look as though you had lost your best friend."

"I am about to," he replied, "unless you go into hiding until time has softened the blow. Caligula is furious. He says that you deliberately threw the race."

"In a way, I did."

"How is that?" asked Numerius. "It was the Red driver who caused the accident; no one else is to blame." Of course Numerius did not know what I had done; he thought that I was just the innocent victim of an accident for which I was in no way responsible. When Tibur told him that I had deliberately fouled the Blue to avoid running him down and that Caesar had lost an enormous wager because of this, he was shocked. For a moment he was silent, only placing his hand upon my arm and pressing it.

Then he said, "There are no words." Nor could any amount of extravagant thanks have as well expressed his gratitude. Presently he turned to Tibur. "What can we do to save Britannicus from the wrath of Caesar?" he asked.

"I can hide him out in the home of my wife's mother until the crazy fool has calmed down or forgotten," said Tibur.

"And get yourself, your wife's mother, and your wife whipped to death or crucified along with me," I said. "No, there is no escape from Caesar, except through Caesar himself. I am going back to the palace immediately and face the music."

I must admit that I had to concentrate assiduously upon the pride and courage of Cingetorix as I made my way to my apartments, which were close to those of Caligula and Caesonia. Here, my slaves awaited me, for, although a slave myself, Caligula had given me slaves to wait upon me—a couple of Ethiopian boys. I asked them if Caesar had sent for me, but they said that he had not, and I breathed more easily for the respite.

I took off my torn and soiled tunic, bathed and dressed again, but still no summons from the tyrant. I sent one of the boys to ascertain if he had returned to the palace. He had not. The suspense increased my nervousness, for I am not made of such iron as can contemplate crucifixion with equanimity.

There came a knock upon the door. It had come! I steeled myself and bade the messenger of death enter. Perhaps Caligula, recalling my long years of loyal service, our boyhood together, had been moved to leniency and was sending a soldier to strike me down, or a slave with poison. Perhaps he would not demand the cross, but, knowing him, I held little hope.

Following my summons, the door opened. I felt my knees go suddenly weak, and I thought I should fall. It was Attica! The reaction left me momentarily dumb.

She ran across the room and threw her arms about me. "Darling!" she exclaimed. Then my knees did truly almost fold beneath me. This was the first word of endearment Attica had ever spoken to me. "Tibur has told me," she said. She pressed her cheek against my shoulder. "Oh, my darling, now you must live! Caesar could not be so cruel. I shall beg Caesonia to plead for you. I will go myself and beg him to spare you."

I had her in my arms. Caesar, the Via Flaminia, nothing else meant anything to me now but this one fact: I had Attica in my arms and I was kissing her mouth. "You love me?" I asked. It was difficult, even now, to believe.

"I have always loved you," she replied. "I was almost sure of it that day when we walked together along the Via Appia beyond the Capena Gate just before you went to Germany. Now I know it. I promised to give you my answer after the races today. You have it."

Again there came a knock upon the door. My brief moment of happiness was over. I realized it as another of Caligula's slaves entered the room. "Caesar demands your presence *immediately*," he said. He emphasized immediately.

"I'll go to Caesonia at once," exclaimed Attica, "and beg her to intercede."

I kissed her and forced a smile. "Wait until she has something for which to intercede. We may just be borrowing trouble." Attica shook her head, for she knew Caesar; but she promised to wait.

Caligula was in a black and furious mood when I entered his presence, and I knew that I could expect only the worst. It would be the Via Flaminia for certain.

"You pig! You blockhead! You fungus!" he screamed at me. "You lost the race so that I would lose five hundred thousand sestertii! How much were you paid? How much did you make out of it, you ingrate?"

"Nothing, Caesar," I said. "You know me better than to think that."

"Then why did you do it? I saw you deliberately swing your team into the path of the Blue."

"I did only what you would have done in my place, Caligula."

"What do you mean?" he demanded.

"I did it to save the life of my friend, who would have been trampled to death had I driven over him."

"He was but a slave," growled Caesar.

"He was my friend."

"Didn't you think of me?"

"I certainly did."

"What did you think? Tell me."

"I thought that you would have me crucified."

Caesar knitted his brows in thought. I imagined that he was debating whether to have me put on the rack before crucifixion.

"Ever since boyhood you have feared the Via Flaminia," he said presently, with a crooked grin.

"As you well know, Caligula."

"Yet you risked it to save the life of a friend."

For some time he was silent. What twisted, malevolent thoughts were passing through his mad brain? Suddenly he burst into that rasping, hideous laugh with which I was so familiar. Now I knew that his decision was made, that my fate was sealed.

"I have it!" he exclaimed. "My wager was with Apponius. I shall have him beheaded and confiscate his estates. I shall thus recover my five hundred thousand sestertii and get his entire fortune in addition. Now get out of here, but see that you never throw another race when I have money on you."

Chapter XX

✠ ✠

EARLY IN January A.U.C. 793, Attica and I, having obtained permission from Caesar, were married. As we were both slaves, the ceremony was a simple one—merely a gesture to satisfy our pride—as marriages between slaves could not be legal under Roman law.

It was, however, remarkable for one circumstance: it amused Caesar to perform the ceremony himself. He even gave a banquet in our honor to which he invited the two consuls, several senators, and other important patricians. Most of these were greatly embarrassed, but they could not refuse the invitation of Caesar, no matter how much they loathed the idea of dining with slaves.

During the meal, Caligula could scarcely keep his eyes from Attica, an attention which greatly perturbed me. Once he turned to me and said, "It is well for you that your wife is not a patrician."

"Why?" I asked.

"Were she, I should take her away from you and marry her myself," he replied.

I made up my mind then to keep Attica out of sight of Caesar as much as possible; if he could take a general's wife away from him, he could certainly take a slave's.

Our honeymoon was of short duration, as Caligula suddenly decided to invade and conquer Britain. As in his other mad schemes, he could brook no delay, and a great expedition was soon formed and on the march. Caesonia and Attica were left behind, the Empress just having given birth to a girl baby which Caligula publicly accepted as his own. Attica told me that even Caesonia could not be certain as to who had fathered it.

We were away for almost a year on this ridiculous venture. Having come at last to the coast of Gaul directly opposite Britannia, Caesar caused his armies to prepare for battle, and they were thus formed, facing the island of my nativity.

I was much excited as the fleet set sail to cross the channel, for now I should soon set foot again upon the soil I loved so well. My only sorrows were that I was coming with an invader and that Attica was not with me.

We had proceeded but a short distance when Caligula gave the order to come about, and the fleet sailed back to Gaul. What had happened, why this was being done, I could not imagine. But who could fathom the strange vagaries of that mad mind!

Upon disembarking, I saw that a throne had been erected near the beach during our absence, and now Caesar seated himself upon it and gave orders that all the trumpeters of the army should sound the attack.

As the stirring call issued from the brazen throats of the trumpets, I could see not only the officers but the men as well looking in all directions for an enemy. The ranking general hastened to the throne and asked whom the army was to attack.

"The sea, of course," shouted Caligula. "Let my army seize the spoils of war in proof of the mighty victory we have won."

"Spoils of war?" questioned the general.

"Certainly, you numskull!" screamed Caligula. "The shells! The shells! The shells! The treasures of Neptune, who has defied me!"

The general looked foolish. He was a veteran of many campaigns. His legionaries looked up to him with respect and awe—and now he had to make himself ridiculous by ordering them to gather shells on the seashore. He delegated this duty to a subordinate and went and hid in his tent, sending word to Caesar that he had been suddenly attacked by sickness.

The soldiers fell to work filling their helmets with shells, amid laughter and coarse joking. It was well for Caesar that they took the whole affair good-naturedly, for incensed Roman legions might well make even a Caesar quail.

Caligula assumed the mien of a stern and ruthless conqueror, swearing great soldier oaths as he urged his invincibles on to further despoilation of the enemy, until his throne was surrounded by great mounds of shells.

"These spoils of Ocean shall be dragged behind my chariot when a triumph shall recompense me for this glorious feat of arms," he announced, "and they shall be reserved for the imperial palace and the Capitol."

At last the silly undertaking was over, largess was distributed to the legionaries, and all returned to camp. Later, Caligula had a lighthouse erected at the spot to immortalize his victory.

Before returning to Rome, he had many tall Gauls brought to him. They were made to learn the German language, clothe themselves like Germans, and let their hair grow long and dye it red. These were to be the captives that were to walk in chains behind his chariot when he enjoyed his triumph. I wondered how he was to explain that he had made only German captives in Britannia. Perhaps no one would ask him—certainly no one would who enjoyed life. I did not.

We were gone from Rome almost a year upon this mad expedition, and when we returned I found that I was the father of a boy—you, my son. Then followed the happiest days that Attica and I had ever known—the happiest that I ever was to know. The only cloud upon our horizon was an occasional indication of interest in Attica on the part of Caligula—an interest which turned her cold from horror but made my blood boil. I am sure that all that kept his foul hands from her was his lifelong subconscious fear of me—a fear implanted deeply within his childish mind that time he had spit upon me and I had slapped him.

Once he said to me, "Do not you, a slave with a beautiful wife, fear lest some man win her away from you?"

"I have no fear on that score," I said. "I trust Attica."

"But suppose some man should take her by force?" he persisted.

"I would kill him," I said.

"No matter who he was?"

I looked Caius Caesar Caligula straight in the eye. "Even if it were Caesar," I said, for I knew what was in his vile mind, and I was willing to risk death in an effort to deter him from that which he was contemplating.

"No other man in all the world dares say to me the things that you are always saying," he grumbled. "I do not know why I let you live." Then he walked away. I breathed more easily, for now I felt that Attica was safe. I thought that I knew my Caligula.

I did not tell Attica of this encounter, but I told Tibur and Numerius, and they both swore that if the worst befell me they would protect Attica with their lives.

"And if he harms her," said Tibur, "I will split the fungus on the same sword that I offered his father."

Numerius said nothing, but the expression on his face boded ill for anyone who might even so much as cast a carnal glance at Attica. I think that no one ever had two better friends than I, in Tibur and Numerius. The fact that I had won Attica never lessened Numerius' friendship for me. I sometimes thought that it had augmented it, since now he felt even more responsible for my welfare on account of Attica. My sole regret concerning these friendships was that Tibur was a Roman, for I admit that my hatred of them verged upon the fanatical. But it was only a regret: it did not lessen my affection for the great gorilla.

Upon his return from the expedition against Britannia, Caligula's excesses against every class of society increased. None was immune except the army, which he greatly feared. He sought to destroy the entire Senate piecemeal and with the most diabolic cruelties.

He decreed the execution of Cassius Bettilinus and commanded his father, Capito, to attend and witness his son's death. I shall never forget the horror and grief depicted upon the old man's face as Caesar issued his commands.

"You may bid me be present," said Capito, "but you cannot prevent me shutting my eyes."

Caligula laughed. "Very well," he said, "you shall die then with your son."

I was forced to witness this execution, as I was forced to witness many others, for Caligula usually kept me near him at such times because he particularly feared assassination. He was not so mad but that he knew that someday one of his victims might turn upon him. Upon this occasion, he had the condemned men's mouths stuffed with sponges, as he often did, to keep them from crying out accusations against him.

Upon another occasion, he invited a knight named Pastor to dine with him following the execution of one of his sons; nor did Pastor dare refuse lest he place in jeopardy the life of another son. Caligula told me to watch Pastor to note if he showed any signs of sadness, and he deliberately made joking remarks at which the poor man was compelled to laugh. When Caesar's eyes were not upon him, Pastor's were filled with anguish, but he might have wept and torn his hair and I would not have informed the monster.

His degradation of the Senate was such as to have brought a blush of shame to the cheek of the most hardened criminal, and augmented the contempt in which the masses had long held that once honorable body. There was, for instance, the abject spectacle of the senator, Pompeius Pennus, a very old man who had held high offices in the State. An accusation had been brought against him, but Caligula had pardoned him. He then compelled the senator to kneel before him in public and kiss his foot. Not content with such humiliations, he caused members of this once august body to assume in public the role of executioner.

Not only had he contrived to turn the knights and senators against him, but by exorbitant taxes he lost the good will of the common people. His taxes upon all foods brought into the city, upon all trades, and upon their amusements as well so enraged the populace that there had been a serious demonstration against him in September of A.U.C. 793, at which time Caligula had set his soldiers upon the crowd, killing and wounding many, severing the last bond of affection they had ever felt for him.

The army, which had for long been loyal to their Little Boots, was disgusted by his silly and cowardly antics in Gaul against the Germans and the Britons. They were ashamed to serve under such an emperor. Thus he had lost his last and strongest ally among his own people. All that was left to him were the German troops which constituted his imperial bodyguard, whose loyalty he preserved by lavish gifts of money and the bestowal of favors. Such was the situation in Rome at the beginning of the 794th year from the founding of the city.

Caligula had become more and more fearful of assassination at the hands of the Senate or the knights, of rebellion of the populace, or of the mutiny and revolt of the army. "They all hate me," he said to me early one morning as, sleepless, he paced the porticoes. "The Senate, the people, the army." And then he repeated that seeming challenge which was but an admission of his great weakness and his great fear: "I care not if men hate me, just so they fear me."

"Caesar, to whom all things are possible, might win back the affections of his people," I suggested.

He looked at me for a long time in silence, until I wondered if what I had said might not bring down upon me the maniacal wrath of the mad tyrant; then he said something which I shall never forget, something which revealed his awareness of his malady: "Were I like other men, I might."

Again there was a long silence, broken only by Caligula's wordless mutterings, as he paced the long porticoes in the first dim coming of the dawn. "I know what the Roman pigs want," he suddenly exclaimed. "They want blood—anyone's blood but their own. They shall have it, and then perhaps they will love me again. I will give them such games as never before were seen: five hundred pairs of gladiators, some on foot, some on horseback, some in war chariots such as your barbarous Britons use. I'll give them fights between wild beasts—tigers against elephants, wild bulls against lions; and there shall be a beast hunt such as no man has ever before dreamed of—the prisons of Rome shall be emptied to fill the arena with men and women to battle against a thousand wild beasts. And if that is not enough——" He broke off and commenced to laugh—that laugh which sent the cold shivers down my spine. What plan was evolving in the distorted convolutions of that warped brain?

With the restless animation which usually marked the accomplishment of each new vagary, he rushed the preparations for the great games to the exclusion of all else, including affairs of state. Had he been preparing to resist an invasion he could not have driven his lieutenants with greater fury. High officers of the army, knights, senators, and even the two consuls were forced to give up all other activities and devote their time to the collection and transportation of wild beasts and gladiators and the housing and feeding of them. Every dangerous beast that could be brought to Rome within the two weeks before the opening of the games was commandeered.

The games were to last five days. The final event upon the fifth day was to be the great beast hunt. The first four days were devoted largely to gladiatorial combats and encounters between pairs of wild beasts pitted against one another, or of individual men against a beast. By the fifth day, the populace was sated. The audience was restless and grumbling. There were hoots and catcalls and demands for the great beast hunt.

As usual. Tibur and I were in the imperial loge. Senators sat at the feet of Caesar, whispering words of praise and affection to the man whom they feared and hated above all other living creatures. Caesonia, being indisposed that day, was not present and so Attica was not with us, but she was in the audience. Some friends had persuaded her to accompany them, and she sat in an unreserved section among other slaves and plebs. She had not wished to attend, as she loathed the brutality of the games, but the importunities of her friends had prevailed.

To my surprise. Caligula evinced no anger because of the restlessness of the audience. His head cocked on one side in that characteristic posture, he sat with a smug grin twisting his lips. He appeared to be awaiting something with evident anticipatory relish.

At last the arena was cleared for the final event of the games—the great beast hunt. Several hundred criminals were herded out upon the sand, both men and women. All were armed: some with swords, some with spears, others with tridents. Many of them carried nets—as futile against wild beasts for either attack or defense as would have been a child's slingshot charged with paper pellets.

"Now they shall have what they have been bellowing for," said Caligula, "and a little later they

shall have more than they bellowed for. They
wanted blood. They shall have it."

I didn't like the nasty grin upon his face. I
wondered what he had in mind. I wondered what
new atrocity he was about to commit. There remained in my memory his maniacal laughter the
morning that he had planned these games. Had I
known what was to come, Caius Caesar Caligula
would have died in his loge that day in the amphitheater of Statilius Taurus.

The poor criminals huddled, terrified, in the center of the arena. Most of them were the scum of the
vicious and degraded lower classes of citizens and
slaves but there were among them political prisoners from the aristocracy—even knights and senators. Thus did Caesar love to degrade and humiliate
those whom he feared or hated.

And now the starved beasts began to be raised in
elevators from the pits beneath the arena. There
were hyenas, wolves, leopards, lions, tigers, bulls,
buffaloes, rhinoceroses, and elephants. They spewed
forth onto the sand in such a bedlam of growling,
grunting, roaring, bellowing, and trumpeting as may
never have been heard since the days of the fabulous Ark of which the Jews tell.

Now the hapless victims milled about like a mass
of maggots, as many of them sought to insinuate
themselves into the center of the crowd in the hope
of thus deferring the dread moment when tusk or
fang or talon should rend them. Men pulled women

back from temporary safety that they might win
this brief reprieve for themselves; but there were
other, braver souls, who stood upon the outer rim
boldly facing the nervous, excited beasts with their
puny weapons.

A gaunt, starved tiger slunk slowly forward. It
was followed by a lion. Men seated upon the arena
wall hurled barbed darts among the other beasts to
goad and infuriate them. A bull charged, impaling a
man upon his horns, tossing him high in air. Women
screamed. Men shouted curses at Caesar.

Now the entire great body of beasts was moving
hither and thither. A lion leaped full into the close-
packed crowd. The wolves circled, darting in to
snap at legs and leap quickly away. A tiger ran
afoul an elephant which lifted it on high and hurled
to the very center of the packed mass of humanity;
then men and women fought to escape the raking
talons of the maddened cat, and the crowd opened.

A rhinoceros, perpetually enraged as are all his
kind, dull-witted, half-blind, charged straight
through the body of the clawing, shrieking victims
like some huge, animated battering ram. Leopards,
perhaps the cruelest and most vicious of all the
great cats, were tearing and rending in pure lust to
kill and maim—spotted Caligulas of the jungles.

I happened to glance at the section where Attica
sat, looking for her, when I noticed perhaps a
century of Caesar's German guards coming down
the aisles from above. I wondered why they were

there, thinking that perhaps there had been a rumor of a contemplated revolt. I was apprehensive on Attica's account, but as I saw no sign of trouble brewing in that, or any other section of the stands, I sought to quiet my fears.

Hearing Caligula laugh that mad laugh of his, I turned to look at him. He slapped a consul on the shoulder. "They wanted blood," he cried, "and they shall have it. They shall have entertainment enough today to last them for a long time!" Then he half-rose and waved his handkerchief toward that section of the stands where the German soldiers were. It was the signal!

Immediately the soldiers began to drive the men and women from that section of the stands down toward the arena. At first, I could not grasp the significance of the act. Even knowing Caligula as well as I did, I could not conceive of the wanton cruelty that was about to be perpetrated upon innocent and helpless men and women upon his orders.

I saw Attica being herded forward with the rest. I stood up to see better. Tibur stood beside me. "What does it mean?" I asked. He shook his head. "I am afraid," I said. "Attica is there."

"Where?" he asked.

"Among those the soldiers are driving from their seats."

The crowd was silent now. Everyone must have been watching that section of the stands that was being emptied by the Germans. Presently the truth dawned upon me as the soldiers began pushing the poor creatures over the wall into the arena.

I almost knocked Caesar from his throne as I leaped toward the front of the loge, stepping full upon the fat stomach of a senator. An instant later and I had vaulted into the arena and was running across the sand toward the spot at which the new victims of Caligula's mad whim were being thrown to the beasts.

How I crossed without being dragged down by some blood-mad carnivore, I shall never know. I do recall that once a leopard barred my way, but I think my impetuous rush must have filled him with consternation, for he leaped from my path and let me pass unscathed.

The other beasts, attracted by this diversion, seemed to be centering their attention upon the newcomers—all but those which were tearing at the bloody corpses of their kills.

Attica must have seen me coming before I located her, for presently I saw her running toward me. And I saw something else that froze the blood in my veins: a tiger, evidently attracted by the running girl, was trotting toward her at my right. It was a question as to which of us would reach her first. I exerted every effort to put speed into my feet, but I was conscious of that sensation of extreme futility which one sometimes encounters in dreams, where one's feet seem to be weighted with lead; yet I did reach Attica just before the tiger.

With drawn sword, I placed myself between her and the striped fury. My sword! A wet rag might have been almost as effective a weapon with which to combat those four hundred pounds of iron sinew and muscle.

The beast reared up on its hind feet to seize me. It towered above me, its great, yellow fangs bared in a hideous, wrinkled grimace of bestial rage, its yellow eyes glaring into mine. I struck at that frightful face with my puny sword, and simultaneously a spear tore into the striped side just behind the left shoulder. Tibur was at my side! He had followed close behind me, picking from the bloody sand of the arena a spear fallen from some dead hand.

The screams of the stricken beast almost deafened me. It lunged to rake this new antagonist with its powerful talons. Only such a giant as Tibur could have held it off, and while he did so, I struck again and again at its now bloody head.

It seemed much longer, but it could have been no more than a few seconds before the tiger sank to the sand, dead; for Tibur's spear had pierced its heart.

Seizing Attica's arm, I hurried her to the side of the arena, Tibur upon her other side. German guardsmen looked down at us. Tibur and I lifted Attica toward them. "Help her up!" I ordered.

They hesitated. "It is a command from Caesar," I shouted.

All these German guardsmen knew both Tibur and me at least by sight. They knew that we were both close to Caligula and that Tibur was a tribune of the guard. They reached down and drew Attica to safety; then they helped Tibur and me to scale the wall.

The audience was in a state of confusion, bordering almost upon riot. I could hear cries of "Shame!" "Murder!" "Down with Caesar!" All were standing. Hundreds were jamming the exits in an effort to escape the amphitheater before the crazy young tiger had others hurled to the beasts.

The great Tibur shouldered his way through the angry, frightened, milling crowd, and Attica and I followed in his wake. It took us a long time to make our way to the exit, but at last we were in the open. As we emerged from the amphitheater and made our way up the hill toward the palace, we saw Caligula, escorted by two centuries of German guardsmen, hurrying ahead of us. We learned later that he had become terrified by the threatening attitude of the people and fled.

By the time we reached the seclusion and temporary safety of my apartments, Attica was in tears. "You will both die for this," she sobbed. "I am not worth it."

I tried to reassure her that, after all, we had done nothing to arouse the wrath of Caligula and that we were in no danger, but I knew better and so did she and so did Tibur. Once again the shadows of the crosses along the Via Flaminia fell across me.

But days passed and nothing happened. Caligula was sour and morose, for he was frightened; yet he did not punish us. He did not even mention the thing that we had done. Later, Cassius Chaerea, a tribune of the guard, told me something which explained why Caesar's wrath had not fallen upon Tibur and me. Caligula had been much excited and intrigued by our exploit. He said that it had added the final touch to the excitement of the beast hunt, affording a splendid finale to the games. "Had I planned it myself, it could not have been better," he said, and then he added, "I would have ordered them down myself to rescue the girl had I known that she was among those thrown to the beasts. She is too beautiful to be wasted thus."

So Caesar was still thinking of the beauty of my wife!

Chapter XXI

A.U.C.794 [A.D. 41]

✠   ✠

TOWARD THE middle of January, word of a plot
against his life was whispered to Caligula. The
senator, Pompedius, who, it later developed, was
not in any way connected with the plot, had heard
of it, and, like the fool that he was, had repeated the
rumor to the actress, Quintilia, a famous beauty.
Pompedius was arrested upon another charge, and
Quintilia was sent to Cassius Chaerea, tribune of
the guard, to be placed upon the rack in an effort to
force a confession from her.

At that time it was not known to me that the plot
was real and that Chaerea was the instigator of it.
This man, a soldier of repute, had grown gray in the
service of the Caesars. He had known and loved
Little Boots when the latter was a child in the
camps of the Roman legions in Germany, but grad-

ually his loyalty had been undermined by the cruelties and excesses of the mad Caesar. His growing hatred of the tyrant was further increased by personal insults and ridicule heaped upon him by Caligula.

Chaerea had a shrill and slightly feminine voice, which Caligula would mimic for the purpose of ridiculing the tribune before his fellow officers and even in the presence of common soldiers. Perhaps it was these personal insults which determined Cassius Chaerea to rid the world of the mad monster.

I was present with Caesar when Quintilia was tortured upon the rack. Before the girl was brought in by the soldiers, Chaerea must have been filled with fear that her confession would implicate him; but, and this I learned later from Chaerea himself, when Quintilia passed him in the torture chamber, she pressed a foot upon his and gave him a quick, reassuring glance.

Among all the horrors that I witnessed during the reign of Caius Caesar, the torturing of Quintilia upon the rack seemed to me the most horrible. I wish that I could forget it. Under the eyes of Caesar and upon his insistent commands, Chaerea was forced to subject the girl to the most excruciating agony, but no word of confession could be forced from her lips, and at last the cruel dislocation of her joints aroused a faint spark of compassion even in the stony heart of the tyrant. He commanded Chaerea to cease, and after leaving money for

Quintilia, quit the torture chamber. No evidence having been elicited against Pompedius, he also was later discharged. I imagine that Cassius Chaerea must have nearly fainted from relief.

Caligula seemed to forget the rumored plot during the preparation for the Palatine games, a festival sponsored originally by Livia in honor of the founder of the monarchy. The games began on January 17th and ended upon the 24th. To house them, an enormous wooden theater was erected at the foot of the Palatine.

January 24 A.U.C. 794 dawned like any other Roman winter day. It was the last day of the games, upon which several plays were to be performed. In one there occurred the capture and crucifixion of a robber chief, in which a criminal was to be forced to play that part and to suffer actual crucifixion upon the stage. I was glad, therefore, when Caligula dispatched me upon an errand that would keep me from the games that day. I had no desire to see a man crucified.

While he had been in good spirits that morning, yet he appeared even more restless and nervous than usual. He complained of Caesonia, of whom he was tiring, and spoke of ridding himself of her and taking another wife. "This time I shall really surprise the world," he exclaimed. "I shall give the miserable Roman mob an empress such as it deserves," and then he laughed that hideous, mad laugh which always portended some new extravagance or cruelty.

The errand upon which he sent me to his villa in the country seemed most trivial to me. The lowliest of his slaves might have as well performed it, and as I rode along the highway in the bright winter sunlight, I speculated upon the reason that had induced him to send a trusted protector from his side at a time when he would be publicly exposed to the swords and daggers of his enemies. I shall always curse myself for the stupidity which kept me from suspecting his real reason and blindly assuming that he was motivated by some trivial vagary of his diseased brain—perhaps a mean desire to prevent my witnessing the last and principal events of the games. Caligula was as capable of such petty meannesses as of the most fiendish cruelties. I think that one might have counted upon the fingers of one hand all of the acts of kindness and generosity which he had performed during his lifetime and for which he had not demanded repayment many times over, as, for example, the several occasions upon which he had given a momentary favorite a huge donation and then ordered his execution and confiscated his entire estate.

That which happened in the city between the time that I left and my return in the evening I may only recount from hearsay. Many of the reports were contradictory, but I shall set down here that version which appears most plausible and which had the greatest number of vouchees.

At the theater that day, Caligula was, of course, seated in the imperial box, which was to the left of the stage. The captain of the Praetorian Guard, Vatinius, sat directly behind the Emperor; and the consul, Pomponius, at his feet; nearby was Cluvius, a man of consular rank.

Pomponius turned to Cluvius and said, "How now, friend? Any news today?"

"None that I have heard," replied Cluvius.

"Do you not know that today's play depicts the slaughter of a tyrant?"

"Hush!" whispered Cluvius. "Beware, my friend, lest others hear thy tale."

"And the day—what day is this?" asked Vinicianus in a low voice.

"It is that on which Philip of Macedon was slain by Pausanius, my friend," replied another senator.

And a third added, "At the play!"

It was obvious that the plot was by now an open secret, and only the fact that Caius Caesar Caligula had no friend left could account for his remaining unwarned. Among all the favorites, sycophants, and trusted officers about him there was not one but would have been glad to see him dead. Was there one with the courage to kill him?

The consul, Pomponius, lying at the Emperor's feet, stooped occasionally and kissed the gilded slippers of the tyrant. A noble Roman, Pomponius! Yes, quite as noble as they come.

On preceding days, Caligula had left his box and returned to the palace for the midday meal. Believing that he would do so this day, Chaerea had left the theater and was lying in wait to assassinate the Caesar as he passed between the theater and the palace; but today Caligula decided to have luncheon served in the imperial box, and sent for food.

Vinicianus, who was one of the plotters, feared that this change in the plans of Caligula might result in the failure of their attempt, and wishing to warn Chaerea, he rose to leave the theater. Caius, seeing him stand up, took hold of his toga. "My good fellow," he said, "where are you going?"

Vinicianus was embarrassed. He mumbled some incoherent reply and reseated himself. But his anxiety increased. He knew that if the assassination were too long delayed, word of the plot might reach the ears of the Emperor—too many now knew of it, and among Romans one seldom knows whom one may trust.

At last, at a moment when Caesar's attention was directed elsewhere, Vinicianus left the theater. He found Chaerea at the doorway.

"All is ready," said the tribune. "I have posted loyal men all along the way, but why has Caesar not come?"

When Vinicianus explained the change in Caligu-

la's plans, Chaerea said that he would return to the
theater and strike him down in his box.

Vinicianus attempted to dissuade him. "There
would be a riot," he said, "perhaps a general fight
and massacre. Don't forget Caesar's German bodyguard. Those wild barbarians would like nothing
better than to get their swords into a few-score
Roman bodies."

While the two plotters were arguing, Asprenas, a
senator who was also one of the conspirators, became more and more uneasy because of the change
in Caesar's plans. He had seen Chaerea and Vinicianus leave the theater, and he sought some excuse
by which he could persuade the Emperor to return
to his palace. At last he whispered to Caius that he
must be tired and that, as the great spectacle of the
day could not take place until after dark, it might
be well for him to return to the palace. "After a
bath and a meal," he urged, "Caesar will be better
able to enjoy the performance."

"Perhaps you are right," replied Caius. "I shall
do so."

A procession was formed with old Claudius,
Caligula's uncle, Marcus Vinicius, the husband of
the banished Julia, and Valerius Asiaticus at the
head. Outside the theater Chaerea and Vinicianus
joined the procession, which was composed of
officers of the guard and men of prominence.

Quite unexpectedly, Caius turned sharply into a
long gallery that led to the bath-house, leaving his

uncle and the others at the head of the procession to continue by the ordinary way.

In the gallery, Caius met a party of boys from Greece and Asia Minor, who were to perform in the final scene of the theater. Caius stopped to talk with the boys and was inclined to turn back with them. Their manager, however, begged that they be permitted to go and warm themselves, as they were cold. Caesar assented and started on toward the palace. He had taken but a few steps when Chaerea approached and asked him for the watchword. The dancing boys and their manager were still there as Caligula gave Chaerea an ugly word, imitating the old tribune's high-pitched voice; and as he did so, he made an insulting gesture—all to win a laugh from dancing boys at the expense of an officer of the Praetorian Guard.

Chaerea whipped out his sword. The time had come!

I must have reached the palace on my return from the summer villa of the Emperor about the time that Asprenas was suggesting to Caesar that he return to the palace. I went directly to the apartments occupied by Attica and myself. As I crossed the threshold, I passed from a life of happiness and hope to one of hopelessness and despair: Attica lay upon the floor in a pool of her own blood!

I rushed to her side and knelt. Both her poor wrists were slashed deep. She looked up at me and tried to smile. I took her in my arms.

"Caesar," she whispered, and then she died.

All the hatred and contempt for the madman that I had kept pent up within me for all the long years surged through me now, doubled, trebled by this last hideous act of his. But it would be his last! That I swore above the dead body of my poor Attica as I laid it gently upon a couch; then I ran from the palace toward the theater with one all-consuming thought driving me on: at last I should kill a Caesar!

It chanced that I took the way along which Caligula had elected to return from the theater, and I came upon him just as Chaerea's sword struck the monster between the neck and shoulder. The blade struck the collarbone, and Caius staggered back; then he turned to run up the passage, and I met him, sword in hand.

"Britannicus!" he screamed. "Save me!"

"For Attica!" I said, and ran him through.

He fell to his knees, and Cornelius Sabinus thrust his sword into him. Somebody dealt him a blow that cleft his jaw. He sank to the marble floor then and drew his limbs together, screaming, "I am alive! I am alive!"

The conspirators gathered around, hacking at him with their swords, crying, "Again! Again!" Had it been any but the mad monster they thus mutilated, it would have been horrible; but, because it was he, to me it was a sweet sight, though I did not touch him again with my sword after that one thrust.

The screams of the dancing boys and some slaves brought the German guard, but before they arrived the conspirators had dispersed. Bowed with sorrow, I returned to my dead. I think that all that supported me was the knowledge that I had avenged Attica and, at last, done that which I had long dreamed of doing—killed a Caesar.

My quarters adjoined those of Caligula. As a boy I had slept on a mattress at the foot of his bed; later I had slept just outside his door, but in an apartment of my own. Practically all of Caligula's life I was within call both day and night. Now he was dead. My hand had helped to kill him. I felt no regret, other than that I had not struck long before—when I first realized his carnal interest in Attica.

As I sat brooding beside her body, I heard a commotion in the apartment of Caesar. Could it be that he still lived and that they had brought him here! I rose and went to the door that separated our apartments. As I pushed it open, I saw Caesonia kneeling in the center of the chamber. Julius Lupus, a tribune, stood over her with a drawn sword. "Strike!" said the Empress, bending her head downward. "Strike and get it over!"

The sword fell, and the head of Milonia Caesonia rolled upon the marble floor. Then the tribune stepped to a small couch on which lay Julia, the

infant daughter of the woman. He seized the child
by the feet and swung it heavily against the wall,
dashing out its brains. Sickened, I turned away and
closed the door—closed it forever upon the past
after twenty-five years in the palaces of the Caesars.

Late that night, Tibur and Numerius came to me.
In some way they had heard that Attica was dead.
Tibur told me that there was a rumor that I was
known to be one of those who had attacked Caligula.

"They will have to kill someone for this," he said,
"and a slave would be their natural prey. Come
with me. I'll hide you."

"You are a good friend, Tibur," I said. "There
could be none better. You may be sure that I'll not
risk the life of such a friend by making him a party
to my crime. What a friend you have been to me,
Tibur, ever since I was a boy! I have only one
regret."

"What is that?" he asked.

"That you are a Roman."

I thought that Tibur was going to explode. "Who,
in the name of all the gods," he cried, "told you that
I was a Roman? I'm a Greek."

"And all these years I have been feeling sorry for
you," I said.

I have not the heart to write more, my son. What
followed the assassination of Caius Caesar Caligula

in the twenty-ninth year of his life and the fourth of his reign, you may read in your history books—probably greatly garbled, as is all history.